WOLFTRAP

Caltraine is a card shark on the run when he flees Prescott, Arizona with a $10,000 price on his head for murder.

He comes to Pine Knot with an alias and high hopes of getting away from the long — and wrong — arm of the law. His luck improves when gorgeous Terry Armbruster hires Caltraine as foreman at Wolftrap, a ranch prized for its river in cattle country. But Pine Knot's Sheriff Ben Flake doesn't think highly of Caltraine and wants him gone, especially after hearing of the murder charge.

Sheriff Flake organizes a stampede to box Caltraine in Wolftrap. It'll take a showdown — and a few discoveries — to make Caltraine a free man.

WOLFTRAP

Nelson Nye

GUNSMOKE

First published by Robert Hale Ltd.

This hardback edition 2002
by Chivers Press
by arrangement with
Golden West Literary Agency

ISBN 0 7540 8193 1

British Library Cataloguing in Publication Data available.

Printed and bound in Great Britain by
BOOKCRAFT, Midsomer Norton, Somerset

WOLFTRAP

1

The desert played out at the foot of the grade—not the first broiling hell he had managed to cross in three savage weeks of hard riding travel, but certainly the last he'd any hankering to encounter. That he still had water was mainly because he'd not gone at this blind, despite that frantic and sudden departure.

That the time might come when he'd have no choice but to cut and run had ever been one of the hazards of his calling, and Pine Knob had stayed at the back of his mind. A gone-to-seed cowtown kept alive by a mercantile business outfitting prospectors prowling the wastes between Ajo and Tubac, accustomed enough to comings and goings that one more strange face might pass practically unnoticed.

He did not expect to stay there forever. Just long enough, he thought, to let some of the heat fall out of the furor stirred up by that bastardly killing and the ten thousand dollars Broach had put on his head.

A kind of wry humor tugged at the look of Caltraine's heat-flushed face.

Working the riverboats had not been the sinecure some folks imagined, but his recent sojourn in the reestablished capital city of Prescott bade fair by far to prove the costliest months he had put in anyplace.

Not cashwise perhaps. He had found out now that cash wasn't everything. There were still a few binds not amenable to what a man had in his wallet.

He had a right to feel jumpy, he reminded himself. His gut felt like it was filled with fiddle strings. A fugitive's harassments had considerably diminished the cool philosophy that in other times had so well stood between himself and the volatile natures of people he brushed elbows with. All the cultivated calm and ordered run of convictions he had lived by for years had in a matter of seconds been pretty well jarred out of him. Once more, reluctantly, he slanched a look behind.

Night hadn't yet come down so strongly as to shut out altogether the pale sands he'd left his horsetracks on but too thick was the gloom to pinpoint motion more than a short stone's throw away. He could feel his sweat and the crawl of his skin brought on by the notion of unseen eyes which he knew in more reasonable passes of judgment to be extremely unlikely.

Arizona was still frontier enough to give a man plenty of room to get lost in and he had been at some pains to confuse pursuit before he had ever dropped into the brush to unreel his trail through rocky barrancas, spreading it through flint sharp stretches of malapi, running it thinly across windswept ridges, trying every dodge a hard lifetime had taught.

No son of a bitch was going to send him to Yuma!

He was still gambler enough to know that what would be was going to be, but rebellious enough to hope he might beat it. He may have been known as "king of the high rollers'' but he had not always made his living from cards. He'd driven jerkline string for a freight operation and, over in New Mexico, put in some time punching cows for the Bells—even taken one hitch as scout for cavalry before he'd found out there were easier ways. He was no damned dude!

Nor—after three weeks of riding—did he even resemble one.

He showed the burly strength that came from big bones. Tan from exposure overlay the normal pallor indigenous to his profession. With those brawny brawler's shoulders he appeared capable enough despite his less than six feet that most hard losers, after scowling looks, deemed it safer to contain the ugly words they would have spoken.

Long full lips and a heavy nose projected a no-nonsense mien quite in keeping with anything glimpsed in that smolderous stare. Shorn of moustache and sideburns he looked what he was. A fairly tough hunk of man that, in shieldfronted shirt, boots and brushclawed Levi's, could have gotten a handout at any of the dozens of ranches he'd passed.

No woman would ever have called Caltraine handsome, yet there was that about him—some animal magnetism or monolithic aura—which had impelled not a few to accept risks inconsistent with the dictates of good judgment; and each time his thoughts spewed up complaisant Vera he knew himself for seven kinds of a fool.

Impulsive, sometimes reckless, the element of danger had ever been a stimulant. From the very outset it was this which had lent such piquant zest to their adventures. Of course he'd known who she was—rings on her fingers, pictures in the papers; he'd even shared her contempt, scornfully grinning at looks of shock and outrage on the several occasions he had squired her in public.

Caltraine sighed. He should have known a card shark couldn't flout a woman of Vera's prominence at a Governor's Ball and think to carry it off without reprisals. Even had Broach been minded to ignore it, the moguls round him would have howled for Caltraine's scalp. Putting horns on a governor was too much for them to stomach.

In the shouts and confusion that rang through his head he couldn't even be sure he had killed the damn fool. The only sure constant was the fact of the reward, offered dead or alive.

His wasn't the only gun that had spoken in those action crammed moments just before he'd got out of there, but his was the one they had blamed the corpse on. The whole trumped-up deal had an odor of politics he found unmistakable. But that didn't butter any parsnips now. Ten thousand greenbacks would buy a mort of bullets.

Scowling his disgust, Caltraine moved up the grade. It had occurred to him this morning he'd have done better coming into Pine Knob as a prospector. It would have given him more freedom; hiring out to some ranch meant restriction of movement. If he went into this burg as a riding man he was going to be stuck with a riding job. No two ways about that.

So he presently got down and, not much liking it, proceeded to strip his bay gelding of gear. Turned loose, the puzzled animal peered at him curiously as he went into the scrub to hide his accouterments.

When he finally moved off, the freed horse followed, impervious to insults. Not until he'd flung a couple of rocks did the horse, shaking his head with a snort, shy away.

Afoot in strange country was scarcely a fix any man on the dodge could regard with equanimity. It bothered Caltraine, too, but seemed the lesser disadvantage. The town, by his reckoning, had to be someplace up ahead. Pulling the slack from his belt, he dug in his toes, having nothing to carry but his canteen and Winchester.

Sand and greasewood, pear and cholla, began to give way to thickets of bean-hung mesquite and pungent huisache which in turn, as the trail climbed into the up-thrust hills, were replaced by shaggy juniper and piñon.

If he had this straight in his mind, Pine Knob lay in the first fold of mountains facing this way. Before very long he saw the scattering of lights down a long sweep of bench with the hills rising back of it in irregular steps and tumbled contours to a pine-timbered pass.

He'd been through here once; not likely anyone would remember him. Place didn't look to have grown a great deal. Turning the bend past Togelmeyer's corral, he faced the main length of the town's single street and it was like coming home—a place where nothing happened.

Swinging round, he went up the smelly ramp that took him into the stable. He saw a middle-aged man half asleep on a keg against the far wall, alongside a ladder that went into the loft.

Not many prospectors, he guessed, moved around in boots, but at least he had thought to take the spurs off them. He didn't quite know how to explain being afoot to a man well-acquainted with the habits of desert rats. He didn't think that breed was the kind to lose burros.

"Wake up, old man!" Caltraine growled.

Togelmeyer jerked, glowered and settled back. "Just restin' my eyes," he grumbled. "You in some kind of rush?"

"Some son of a bitch while I slept last night slit my burro's throat and packed off about half of him!"

"Damn thievin' Injuns," the liveryman grumbled. "Gittin' worse alla time. Nolla's trash, like enough." He pushed himself up with sundry groans and grimacings, considered the prospect with his head to one side. "How high you figgerin' t' go to replace him?"

"Let's see what you've got," Caltraine countered,

following the trader toward the back door. Just before passing through, the oldster reached up and took down a lantern.

In the end, after much haggling, it was a mule Caltraine settled for, a ginger-colored hinny with one blue eye, which the old man straight-faced told him answered, when it suited, to the name of General Crook.

Neither principal in this transaction appeared greatly impressed with the possibilities, but it was in Caltraine's mind if his situation deteriorated he would sooner pin his chances on this ugly specimen than any pint-sized burro.

After the price had changed hands Togelmeyer snapped a cotton shank to the General's halter and Caltraine, towing him, moved off toward the light-dappled center of town.

He needed an outfit. Next to his skin was a belt crammed with banknotes he'd no intention of taxing. A prosperous prospector would attract too much interest.

They passed three saloons, a bake shop and saddlesmith's, Caltraine pausing finally before a paintless shiplapped building bearing a two by ten sign which, though nearly illegible, spelled out the word: MERCANTILE.

Tying the mule, he mounted the steps and, mindful of his pose, accosted a pair of whittlers hunkered on bootheels just back from the light coming through the open door. "Don't reckon you know where a feller could pick up a grubstake?"

He could feel hard stares lift to rummage his face.

The nearer was a blocky bear of a man in batwing chaps, a chin-strapped hat and a hung-open vest. He had a wad of tobacco locked into his cheek and gruffly said without bothering to spit, "Try inside," and went on with his whittling.

"Thanks," Caltraine said, and moved into the store.

The place was stacked and festooned with a variety of

goods about equally divided between ranching needs and paraphernalia of interest to desert rats. He observed two clerks, both waiting on persons slow to make up their minds.

Caltraine, drifting toward a gun rack, was reminded he was close to being out of rifle fodder. Debating the wisdom of replenishing his stock, balancing possible need against a wary reluctance to disclose such a lack, he was somewhat startled when a voice said behind him, "Yes, sir! Something I can do for you?"

Caltraine, settling into his part again, turned to consider with some astonishment a pigtailed face that in color and mobility most nearly resembled a mask of weathered bronze. The man stood, tall for an Oriental, with hands tucked into the sleeves of his jacket, inscrutably patient.

When Caltraine appeared at a loss for words the descendant of Confucius smiled politely. "You are surprised to find a Chinese proprietor?"

Caltraine rubbed his jaw. "Just a mite. I was looking for a grubstake."

"What do you require?"

It put Caltraine rather back on his bootheels. "I guess" —he shrugged—"about most everything," and told his story of the nonexistent burro, allowing the theft likely some of Nolla's work, enlarging the picture to include loss of camp gear before it occurred to him to wonder what possible use an Indian could have for a pick or shovel.

Perhaps the store owner, too, found this a bit strange, his slant-eyed stare passing blandly over canteen and rifle.

"I am called Wong," he said, inclining his head. "Make a list of your needs and bring it to my office." With a gracious bow, hands still up his sleeves, he went slap-slapping off toward the back of the store.

Caltraine, blinking, stared after him, baffled. Of two minds now, he stood a while, pondering. An Indian would have to be out of his mind to pack off a pick in place of a rifle. Even a dude ought to savvy that much! Yet Wong, though he didn't look stupid or crazy, was apparently willing to let this roll by and invest some of his substance in a man he had never set eyes on before.

It didn't make sense. Not Caltraine's kind.

Things that puzzle a man generally tend more or less to be regarded with suspicion and Caltraine's distrust found plenty to feed on. How many Chinese could you dig from your head as being proprietors of a mercantile business?

Still . . . a man putting money in grubstakes takes his profit from the law of averages. Same as most gamblers. You don't pick marks like winners at a horse show.

Something further was needed to dissipate Caltraine's disquiet. Toting up the chances, he felt more than a little minded to jump on his mule and dig for the tules. The smell of this place was strangely unlike the feel of it he'd carried all these months in his head.

Not being clairvoyant and all too aware of his need for a cover, he grumpily borrowed a paper sack and pencil from one of the clerks and, having made out his list, wandered off toward the rear on a hunt for the man who had offered to stake him.

2

Wong's living quarters were separated from the area of public domain by a stacked-up wall of crates and boxes at either flank of a bead-draped opening through which Caltraine passed to find his man in steel-rimmed spectacles bent over a battered rolltop desk.

"You have your list?"

Caltraine handed it over.

The merchant bent nearer to the light to examine it. "Two months supplies," he remarked, looking up. "Put your name on this, please."

Caltraine wrote *Vic Walters* across the bottom of the list and returned it

Wong blandly asked, "Were you planning to pack all these things on your back?"

"I managed to scrape up the price of a mule."

"You'll need a pack saddle."

Caltraine shifted weight. "I hate to run up a bigger bill than I have to."

"Commendable," Wong said, "but hardly in character." His stare turned reflective. "Your hands tell me, Walters, this prowling you contemplate is something outside your present experience. I have no wish to pry but as your prospective partner I think you should know that the Indians you mentioned are much more efficient than you appear to imagine."

Caltraine's taciturn glance told him nothing.

Wong smiled. "You look like a pretty good risk at that. If you don't find anything of marketable value I suppose one could always get it out of your hide."

"One could try," Caltraine said, and Wong chuckled.

"When do you want to pick up these things?"

"If they're on that platform out back of your place by three in the morning that will be soon enough."

Scouting his way past ragged islands of merchandise, ignoring the rumbles of conversation, Caltraine stepped casually out on the porch, there stopping a moment to put together a smoke.

The blocky whittler in chaps had taken himself off, but against the far end, a blacker shape in the shadows, someone lounged wrapped in silence above the glint of a rifle.

A night wind moved over the street with its odors of dust and a resinous pungence of pine and wood smoke and Caltraine pulled these rank flavors deep into him, let tobacco and paper flutter out of his fingers while he thought his dark thoughts and raked the night with his stare.

Several cat-still shapes stood without talk beneath a pair of tall cottonwoods, the bulk of their interest plainly skewered toward him. Pedestrian traffic appeared at a standstill yet the town had not emptied; there were a lot more hats in the round-about shadows and beneath the board awnings than Caltraine remembered having seen while on his way in.

Tension crawled up his back. The plain feel of danger was a chill in the breeze plucking sound from the eaves.

Three men stepped out of the Kentucky Bar, the one in the middle throwing out both arms to halt his companions while his twisting face slashed quick looks up and down. This was the blocky whittler, who had answered Caltraine's question.

The hairs began to curl at the back of his neck.

Two-thirds of the way down the length of this street a stage, all hitched, stood ready to go and Caltraine, with anger tightening his nerve ends, wondered what chance he stood to get on it.

Under the cottonwoods a man stirred restively. Three doors down, another, rounding a corner, flung himself back out of the light, flattening against the handiest wall.

Alongside a barber's pole someone lifted a hand to tug at his hat brim and on the Carriage House balcony another —in plain sight from Caltraine's position—rose up with a carbine to move into a less cramped stance.

Caltraine reckoned he'd be lucky to reach the bottom of these steps.

Tautly placed, thoroughly still, he considered the street through the cracks of hard eyes, seeing no way of beating this trap. If he tried to whirl and get back inside that fellow staked out in the porch-end shadows could sure as hell cut the legs from under him.

The shocking fright, the wild and desperate churn of his thoughts and hopes that could find no outlet, held him at bay like an immobilized cougar, straining, scarce breathing, anchored in the awareness that time had run out.

The gent by the barber's pole, hunching forward a little, stretched forth an arm and the slice of his hand inclined toward the blackness where, moments earlier, that hurrying shape had ducked out of sight to stand plastered against a gloom shrouded wall.

Between table sessions in the loneliness of idle hours, Caltraine had sometimes considered the bleak aspect of his future when his marriage to cards might no longer suffice. Such occasions he envisioned a woman who had no counterpart but was put together and nourished by dreams. Brown eyed, red lipped, of stillness and depth with hair that ran smoothly away from her forehead, her speaking voice filled with indescribable melody.

He hadn't ever been rightly sure of her thinking, certainly had never expected to encounter her; yet the girl who now stepped from the doorway behind him, brushing past unaware on her way to the street, was the epitome of her—the actual, living, breathing image.

A rattle of wheels, the muted rumble of hooves, pulled his glance from the girl to find the stage moving, coming swiftly this way as the whip snaked out above the flattening ears of the four-horse hitch.

With increasing tension Caltraine's stare swept the shadows, trying to find in the night some answer to his problem. And it was then that he realized the true significance of the man on the balcony's changed position. They weren't caring about him—about Blaze Caltraine; it was the one shoving away from the wall they were after.

"Joe! Go back!" the girl cried, bounding into the street.

The stage, at full tilt, was almost abreast when the fellow broke into a desperate run. Flame lanced from the Carriage House sniper's rifle. The girl, with no eyes for the thundering coach, was trying to reach Joe when the off-wheeler struck. She was slammed half around, spinning into the dust as the stage like an avalanche roared on out of town.

Through the settling cloud—with the sound of its progress still loud in his head—Caltraine in shocked horror eyed the two crumpled shapes. With a curse, he was off the Mercantile's steps, running under a red fog of outrage into a suddenly silent street.

He had the girl in his arms, was straightening up, when a voice sharp-edged with authority said: "Put her down."

Caltraine's lifted stare found the burly whittler in front of him. "This girl needs attention." He started to go round but the man again blocked him and Caltraine saw behind that challenging jaw a number of others.

The man, apparently used to obedience, said in his clipped, arrogant way, "You're on the wrong foot, boy. Better get right."

Caltraine peered. Been a long while since he'd been called boy. He didn't care about that or anything else beyond putting this girl in the hands of a doctor. He said impatiently, "The girl's been hurt—" but the blocking man said like Moses on the mount: "I'll take care of her."

Caltraine's temper exploded. "Get out of my way!"

3

Spoken so unexpectedly—so inescapably blunt and provocatively headlong in their implication of open defiance —the words sucked up all sound and motion into a breathless sort of unbelieving stillness.

Here was a man all done with caution, whose uncaring talk constituted a challenge, who had meant it that way and wanted them to know it. The big man was caught by surprise with his guard down.

His wasn't the only mouth fallen open. The fellow just back of him showed a stunned wonder. Then everyone was waiting for Ben Flake to say or do the only thing left in such circumstances. It was the kind of talk no boss man could take if he aimed to hold onto the status quo.

Watching eyes grew avid. The stillness sharpened with an expectancy honed by past examples as the big man, straightening, came out of his astonishment.

But the looked-for roar did not materialize. With his darkening stare searching Caltraine's face, he said, "You're right. Come with me," and swung round, plunging through a jostle of townsmen to strike off, jaws clenched, toward the Carriage House porch.

By the time Caltraine had lowered her, still heavily awkward in her unconscious state, to a horsehair sofa in the hotel lounge, his temper had cooled enough to perceive the foolhardy thing he'd so unthinkingly done. With the doc clucking over her, Caltraine peered again at the man he'd defied and found himself eyeing an unmistakable enemy.

The man looked to be in his early thirties, red haired, hard twisted, with the chest of a gorilla behind the shaped fit of that hung-open vest. With half the town having witness their set-to, he looked not the kind to forgive or forget.

His head came round to meet Caltraine's scrutiny and a slow flush stung the raw slant of his cheeks. His chin jerked doorward. "Reckon I'll have a few words with you. *Alone*," he growled through tobacco-stained teeth.

Caltraine turned and pushed through the crowd that reluctantly opened when the big man stepped after him.

On the porch Flake said, "We'll go along to my office," and Caltraine, considering, wheeled to ask flatly, "By what right do you crack the whip around here?"

The thumbed-back vest showed the glint of a star. "County sheriff—Ben Flake. That good enough for you?"

Caltraine heard the rasp of anger in his voice. Shrugging, he stepped down when Flake pointed the way.

Inside his dingy lamp-lighted office the star packer, shoving a chair from his path, went back of his desk to pull open a drawer that was hock-deep in papers. He dumped a stack on a slide and commenced flipping through them while Caltraine watched with a gnawing disquiet. Handbills these were, dodgers black with bold type, and—while none offered the price Broach had put on his scalp—Flake paused two or three times to hold one up for comparison.

In disgust, he flopped them back in the drawer, leaned a hip on the desk to regard Caltraine dourly. "Looks like you're clean." The admission bothered him. The weight of his enmity puckered his face and the smoldering stare kept picking and prying. "That feller a friend of yours?"

"Never saw him before."

Flake pulled a plug from the pocket of his shirt, tugged off a gnawed end and broke it up with his teeth. "What fetched you here?"

"It's a free country, isn't it?"

"More trash round now than we aim to put up with." The man studied him some more with that thin heated stare. "You got a handle?"

"Vic Walters."

"My advice to you, Walters, is to hunt greener pastures."

Some perverse streak he couldn't wholly account for twisted Caltraine into saying quite as flatly, "My option, Flake," and the lawman nodded.

"Right now it is. Better give it some thought." He worked a stem from his chaw. "Time could run out on you."

Caltraine's eyes met the sheriff's straightly. "Like it did for that Joe?"

"Joe Ambruster had his warning. He knew what kind of game he was in."

"And that girl?" Caltraine said. "Did she know what game dropped her man from a rooftop?"

"He wasn't her man—he *was a goddamn rustling son of a bitch!*"

The sheriff pushed from the desk still filled with his anger and tapped Caltraine's chest with a hard prodding finger. "Now I'll give you an order. Find a job for yourself inside of three days or I'll bury you so deep the pack rats won't find you!"

Caltraine, after thoughtful scrutiny, said, "I've got a job."

"Yeah? Suppose you tell me about it," Flake said around the wad in his cheek. "Which spread are you at?"

"No spread—"

"I thought not."

"Riding jobs aren't the only kind—"

"They are for a ridin' man."

Caltraine took the time to hang onto his temper. He rubbed at his nose and at last said mildly, "I'm a prospector, Sheriff."

Flake's reaction to that was a skeptical grimace. "Since when?"

"Why don't you ask Wong? He's the one grubstaking me."

The sheriff's hard stare was unreadable. It was plain he reckoned this was easily checked. "So I'll save you a trip." Caltraine smiled, fishing his agreement with Wong from a pocket.

Flake looked it over then went through it again. "No date," he said sourly, tossing it back.

Caltraine put it away. "It's got my name on it, though. Wong's, too. What more do you want?"

"I want you out of here—out of this town and out of this county."

The determination in the way he stood, legs spread, granite jaw forward and mouth whitely clamped, left little doubt he meant every word.

Caltraine's cheeks showed a wistful gravity. "Sheriff, be reasonable. I'll get out of your town but when a man's hunting gold he ain't much for noticing boundaries whose markings are confined to a map."

Flake's smile was ugly. "You get yourself a ridin' job, Walters."

4

Outside on the street with the sheriff's ultimatum banging through his head, Caltraine couldn't see that he had any great amount of choice. The man's anger was too fresh, his authority too sweeping, for the wearer of Caltraine's boots to feel at all comfortable in the thought of ignoring it. He steered for the rail where he'd left General Crook.

The ginger colored mule waggled big ears and blew through his nose while peering to see if he'd been fetched any favors. Caltraine scarcely noticed. Climbing scarred steps to the Mercantile's porch he went on through the door into a babel of jaw-wagging.

The relative quiet that fell over the place suggested most of this palaver had been revolving about himself. It wasn't a notion calculated to brighten his outlook. Wong, he saw, was waiting on trade, engaged at the moment with a buxom woman trying nearsightedly to make up her mind between three partial bolts of figured dress goods and two readymades pulled over wire dummies.

It was clear the sheriff—if he couldn't be rid of him—wanted Caltraine where he could be watched. There were other places a man could hole up but none with this number of subtle advantages so handily adjacent to two hundred miles of near-empty desert.

Every fringe hamlet this side of Sonora would be under close scrutiny. A man could push west to Ak Chin, Lukeville or Yuma, but Yuma was host to the territorial prison, and the whole California border all the way north to Topock would have been sealed off by this time. Greatest danger, in Caltraine's mind, would be wrapped around loners of the bounty hunting breed and these would know every hideyhole open to fugitives. For the moment anyway, in spite of this sheriff, he'd be safer right here than any place he could think of.

Caltraine chewed on his lip. With ten thousand dollars up for grabs no place was safe.

Wong came over when he finally was free and Caltraine followed him back to the office. And came at once to the point. "What's the dope on Ben Flake?"

Wong smiled enigmatically, then said, "He's all the law we have. What perhaps you've not yet discovered is that he happens also to be the topdog cattleman, owner of Chainlink. . . . I guess you won't be wanting that grubstake."

Caltraine, getting out tobacco and papers, thoughtfully stared at things not in this room. Absentmindedly putting the makings away, he said, "Why'd she go out there?"

"Scared, I suppose, her papa's scared, too. Very frightened old man."

With a looker like her Caltraine could understand. It fetched the face of the sheriff back into the picture. Scowling, he said, "That dead feller—Joe. Was he really on the rustle?"

"*Quien sabe?* Depends, I'd guess. He ran a few head from a patch of grass over in Wolftrap."

"What's that?"

"Pocket in the hills off back of the rimrocks. Not too accessible. Takes its name from a creek that runs through it." Wong, smiling thinly, presently said, "You might say he was sort of careless in the men he picked for friends."

This brought Caltraine's head up. "Owlhooters?"

"They've not been convicted. Which isn't to say they won't be if Flake gets his hands on them."

For an interval then they stared at each other, Caltraine's look probing, Wong's bland with a taciturn humor. "Dead men," he said finally, "don't talk."

Caltraine banged a big fist into his palm. He stared unreadably at the likeness of a purple dragon matted and framed against the wall behind Wong, presently heaving an audible sigh. "Better find me some saddle gun shells," he said gruffly, and picked up his rifle.

Wong pulled open a drawer, dug out two boxes and pushed them across the top of the desk. When Caltraine made as though to reach for his purse the man waved it away with a murmured, "Allow me. A small extravagance —an offering, really, to the gods of better business."

Caltraine, observing those eyes, broke open the boxes, distributing the contents into various pockets. "Put a burro on my bill and have him waiting with that grubstake. I'll be on my way inside half an hour."

5

General Crook at the end of a leadshank acted like an oversized Saint Bernard on leash, veering first one way, then trying another. That he didn't quite balk was because his new owner scarcely gave him the chance to really get his feet set.

After tying the beast in front of a hash house, Caltraine went in to take on some food. He could not have said afterward what he put into him, being too much engrossed with current events, partially concerned to find the basis of Flake's enmity.

Sure he'd rubbed the man wrong butting into that business—having his way before the whole push—but the sheriff's animosity stemmed, he thought, from things a lot deeper. More personal somehow, more determinedly vindictive than this would account for.

Was it the girl? Was she the real drive behind Flake's ultimatum? With her kind of looks . . .

He found himself scowling. Trouble was what he'd come here to keep out of, and the right name for trouble too often was a woman, as he had learned to his cost in that go-round with Broach. He could not afford antagonisms here, especially of the sort you could get from a sheriff.

He had a second cup of java while picking and poking at it, skittering round like a scarred old hound come upon a fresh wolf den. If a man had the sense to pound sand down a rat hole he would climb on that mule and shake the dust of this place. Quick as he was able.

No amount of sniffing and snuffling was going to change that. Nor did it matter all his plans had been geared to holing up here. The image of a woman built from an empty bed was damn poor excuse—even in the flesh—for picking up chips in another man's game. The unforgettable memory of Ben Flake's eyes was the only thing that should concern him now but he kept reshuffling, looking for a loophole.

Wong hadn't advanced him that grubstake out of charity. Whatever the reason he'd been gambling on something which had nothing to do with Caltraine's best interests. And Caltraine was not Joe's keeper. That the man had been cut down in some kind of squeeze play was too patently apparent, but it wasn't Caltraine's worry. He'd get all the squeeze any man could take care of from that ten thousand dollars Broach had hung round his neck, and the smartest thing he could do about that was to locate a hole and yank it in after him.

He put the rest of the java down where the chills were, dropped a coin on the counter and rejoined General Crook. Staying on here had lost a heap of its attraction. He was untying the mule when five hard fingers latching onto his arm turned him round, stiffening, to face the rummaging inspection of a nervous girl's appraisal.

Seen close up, the way he looked at her now in the light spilling out of that two-by-four restaurant, she didn't so closely resemble the one Caltraine had been carrying all these months in his head. She was comely enough but considerably taller, with the tilt of her jaw almost level with his own.

He wasn't a man who admired tall women. Shapely for sure—you couldn't quarrel with that, nor with those caverns of eyes so darkly probing his stare.

"You the one who picked me up?"

Her low, throaty voice held an edge of insistence he found queerly disquieting without knowing why. Her lips, parted now, showed thin, cramped with tension . . . like the hand that had hold of him.

"My pleasure," he said shortly.

She slanched a look across her shoulder. "What have they done with him?" He measured her concern by that tightened grip.

"The man's dead," Caltraine said. "It won't make him no difference."

"It makes a difference to me!" she cried, harshly bitter.

When Caltraine failed to respond she let go of him. A shaft of wind whirling up off the desert raced the length of the street lifting dust, flapping shutters, roughly tugging their clothes as it shouldered on past. The girl's angry look took on a dark fierceness. "You know why they killed him?"

"I've been told he was a rustler."

The cut of her eyes turned brightly angry. "They had him boxed. If he was a rustler why didn't that gun-handy sheriff arrest him? He was a sick man, mister, trying hard to get out."

Caltraine stirred restively. "Look, miss, I'm sorry, but I had nothing to do with it."

"You had plenty of company. At least you had nerve enough to pick me up, more than can be said for anyone else. Didn't it make you wonder? Ten months ago Pine Knob would have been up in arms if a man had been shot down like Joe. Any number of folks would have rushed out to stop it—but you saw. Not one of them dared lift a finger!''

She peered at him fiercely. ''Doesn't that say something to you?''

''What happened ten months ago?''

''They elected Flake sheriff.''

Caltraine said, ''Ma'am, I'm a prospector. What goes on in this town has nothing to do with me—''

She said through curled lips, ''You'll find out about that if—'' and chopped the rest off.

He looked at her stubbornly, seeing the courtplaster strips but even more plainly the need that kept nudging the stayropes of caution which wanted him out of this. ''What's done is done.''

He touched his hat but she glommed onto him again. ''For Joe it's done but not for the rest of us. You could help if you would. . . .''

He growled, impatient, ''Let's get out of this light,'' and took the rope off the tie rail, hauling the mule into movement as he turned up the street, the girl keeping pace with him.

''They say you defied Flake. The whole town's talking. You're a marked man now—Ben Flake can't afford to forget what you did. Joe isn't the first to wind up on Boot Hill, and he won't be the last. You can't run away from it. They can't afford to let you.''

''Who can't?''

''Sheriff. You challenged his authority. Thing like that—''

Caltraine said angrily, ''What do you want of me?''

He could feel her tenseness. It was in the swing of her, in the search of that stare.

''They hung the rustler label on Joe,'' she said, ''because he homesteaded Wolftrap and wouldn't let go of it. An all-year creek comes down off the mountains. It crosses that basin but goes underground before it reaches

Flake's range. He's run four of Joe's neighbors off their grass but it's no good to him without he gets water. I want you to go out there and keep him from doing it."

He took another good look at her. "You don't want much, do you?"

"You'll be well paid for whatever you do!"

"How many heads he been running out there?"

"It's the water Flake's after. With control of that creek he can divert—"

"That's not what I asked."

"I don't know," she said, frowning. "Joe didn't know either. Last count he had two hundred mother cows, but they've kept him pinned down, pretty well bottled up. I expect they were hoping to starve him out."

"What ax are *you* grinding?"

"Pardon?"

"What's your interest?"

"That place *belongs* to me now. Joe was my brother— I've been taking care of his father, running the Butterfield station for him."

Caltraine's narrowed stare regarded her flatly. "Why'd you say *his* father? Your old man, too, isn't he?"

The girl flushed, said defiantly, "My mother was Ambruster's second wife. He adopted me, gave me his name when they married."

"She's not living with him now?"

"She died when I was six."

"Is he ailing that you have to take care of him? Or did you mean you keep house—"

"He's been flat on his back for the past three months. That's one of the reasons Joe promised me Wolftrap if he got in a bind he couldn't shake loose of."

"What was he doing in town?"

"He's been having a lot of trouble with his stomach—I told you he was sick. Here lately he couldn't seem to keep nothing down."

Caltraine latched onto a number of notions he didn't much care for. He lifted a hand across his unshaven jaw. "How did Flake know Joe was in town?"

She seemed to think about that. "I suppose someone told him."

Caltraine, also thinking, said, "Here's where I leave you," and stepped back a pace to get onto the mule.

He could feel her hard stare. She said: "If you'll keep Ben Flake off Wolftrap you can write your own ticket."

6

He said, exasperated, "I'm not an army!"

"Doesn't need an army. Just someone with guts and a little bit of gumption—I could do it myself if I was free to go out there! Wolftrap . . . it's got just the one entrance, easily defended. Joe's friends will help—"

"If he's already got help you don't need me."

"He's got the four Ben Flake ran off." Her lip curled noticeably. "Once whipped, twice shy. They've got to have someone to hold them in line."

In the shadow dappled street Caltraine turned about to take another sharp look at her. "Just what are you offering?"

"A run for your money," she said to him coolly. "You're a marked man now and, believe me, you'll stay marked. Sooner or later, without a hole to crawl into, you'll wind up like Joe."

He was starting to say he would take his chances when she flexed the fingers of the hand that was nearest and he saw the pale shine of the gun in her fist.

Caltraine, grimly alert after the first wild rush of unreasoning anger, put resentment aside in the cold mathematics of assessing his future. A snub-nosed derringer in a man's view of things wasn't much of a weapon, but coupled by proximity to the evident state of her unstable emotions it suggested a risk too foolhardy to countenance.

He considered the brittle smile thinning her lips, the hard line of jaw as she dipped that sorrel head. "Going out there, you know, isn't the craziest thing you could do. It might even have several advantages not generally listed under tokens of gratitude."

He showed his own meager smile at this proffered blarney, having long ago learned how far gratefulness would take one. The other points raised might hold a reasonable validity.

"You'd be as out of sight there as any place you might prospect," she chucked at him shrewdly while once more serving up that warmed-over grin. "Don't they claim gold's where you find it?"

He despised being pushed but she'd caught up most of the aces and with pictures of Broach and Ben Flake in his head he was not a free agent. "How do I get there?"

She went over the route, throwing in sundry landmarks, weighing him coldly with that speculative stare. "When you've got through the pass you'll see the cliffs Wolftrap is back of. Don't go dashing into that slot. Ride forward boldly, both hands empty and in plain sight. Pull up when you're about a rope's length from the entrance, take off your hat and with your left hand scratch your head. Don't go any nearer till you're properly invited."

A surge of contempt left its track across tight cheeks. "What happens if they decide not to ask me in?"

"That's something you just better hope doesn't happen."

With continued cool scrutiny she turned up a card that packed considerable authority. "By now Ben Flake will know we've been talking. And the surest thing I can say about that is when you ride out there'll be somebody dogging you.''

Her eyes rummaged his face as though gauging his intentions. "If the boys seem suspicious just tell them I sent you.''

She gave him a final look at her teeth. "If you don't get into Wolftrap I'll know you've wound up in some unmarked grave.''

It was ten fifty-three when Caltraine quit town aboard the mule ahead of a mouse colored burro packed with his plunder. With the girl's words sharply etched in his mind he ignored her directions and swung onto the trail he had earlier come in by, passing Togelmeyer's Corral on his right without a glance.

When he came to where he had stripped the bay gelding he got down and stepped warily into the brush to return with his saddle, blankets and bridle which General Crook eyed without noticeable favor. He even went so far as to hump himself up when he felt the surcingle bite into his belly. Caltraine without ceremony kneed the wind out of him, hauled on the trunk strap and locked it in place.

The feel of a saddle improved his temper and while the mule tongued the bit he took a long look around. If he was under surveillance the fact was not evident.

The girl may have lied—could have been mistaken. Riding the short end of this deal like she was made it easy to attribute greater strength or a wider savvy to that star packing Flake than the man rightly rated, but Caltraine wasn't ready to bet much on this. He'd met enough bastards in his travels to realize this sheriff might turn out to be even more loaded with gall than he'd sounded. In the light of his ultimatum it seemed all too probable he would make it his business to have Caltraine watched.

The ginger mule kept a weather ear peeled but apparently heard no more than his master, only noises indigenous to any hill country, bird sounds and cricket chirps, sundry creaks sprung from weight in the saddle. Though they stopped several times and listened intently, Caltraine caught no rumor of stealthy travel.

He could not believe there was nobody out there. He toyed with the presumption that if he were able to get rid of this shadow he could forget the bind that girl had in mind for him and strike off on his own, perhaps angle toward Ajo and—losing his tracks out there in the desert—try to stay out of sight till the worst of the fever raised by that bounty had worn itself out.

As an exercise it was a pretty fair time passer, but as something to do it had a pretty grim drawback—a two-legged one that wore breechcloth and feathers. Caltraine wasn't one to try fooling himself. Some of these tribes were still pretty hostile. It was easy enough coming in the way he had but trying to get out wasn't quite the same thing. He knew no man could get very deep into desert without having Indians camped on his shirttail. Mule and burro aside, the two months' supplies he'd picked up at the Mercantile would make him stand out in those wastes like a drunk sheep-herder at a parson's box social.

With an irritable grunt he hauled the mule half around, then a little bit more just to prove he could do it, and with a mind not settled peered into the northwest.

He kicked the mule into motion, widely skirting the town as he climbed through low hills, quartering the night for signs of pursuit while hunting the first of the landmarks she'd mentioned. He still wasn't more than half minded to go but without any better destination at the moment he guessed he might as well have a look at that country.

While he rode, cleaving the gloom at a gingerly walk, he kept sifting the things he'd been told, scowling bleakly. Seemed considerably possible the fellow who'd been shot was what he'd been called, a jasper some careless about other folks' cows. He reckoned the girl's talk of water might likewise be true, but what a man in his boots mostly needed right now was a place where for a while he could drop out of sight. She could even be right he wouldn't find any better.

But Wolftrap was a name he found pretty hard to like.

Nor did he very much care for what she'd said about access. He was one who preferred two doors, and the place that guy had come from was too remindful of a box—the kind of box they furnished when a man was buried from town.

Up ahead he could glimpse the first mentioned milestone, a lopsided butte rising tall from the shadows, the spirelike top all but lost against the glimmery look of cold lonesome stars.

Flake had told him to get a riding job and wasn't this just what the girl had offered? A job riding herd on Wolftrap's water.

Be worth something, he reckoned, to see that walloper's face when they fetched him the news Caltraine had taken this job. But against this was the mighty good chance it might be easier to get in than get out of that pocket.

He rode another hour, passing more of the things she had told him to look for before, some disgusted, he told himself this deal wasn't for him.

He saw a pass up ahead climbing through heavy timber. And the wagon track she'd mentioned waggling off to the south just this side of the rise. He was reining the reluctant head-shaking mule between weed-grown tracks when the cry of an owl thinly sheared the blue stillness.

7

Caltraine's thighs grabbed the mule's barrel like the jaws of a vise. Then, knee lifting, he was falling, dropping backward, waist muscles twisting as the leg cleared saddle.

He struck the ground rolling, barely ahead of the slug-churning clamor that beat like near thunder against distant cliffs. Rifle stock hugged, he came onto both knees, the pressure streaked angles of his face harshly sharpening as flexing finger found and closed about trigger.

With wide open eyes he waited, a motionless blotch in windblown shadows that edgily swirled through the night's curdled gloom. Someplace back of him the burro snorted, nervously held by a clutch of rope, fretfully anchored by the mule's greater bulk.

No creeping shape met his searching stare, yet a knowledge of peril built up inside him with gnawing conviction. The strength of this feeling pulled his ducked chin half across his right shoulder. He considered the burro, the stance, the twisted head.

Following the point of rigid ears, Caltraine surveyed a blacker dark topped by a flutter of wind-tossed branches that lifted and pitched in a confusion of shadows.

He'd no real chance to pin anything down and, abruptly aware of this, came full around. Tight-lipped and angry, he put the blunt snout of his reloaded repeater at an angle of readiness, all senses cocked.

Even then he was fooled.

Misdirected by the burro's interest in transportation left tied by the stalker, Caltraine—like the animal—continued to watch the stirring of branches at the thicket's black heart. The slug, when it came, ripped from the dark forty feet to the right.

Caltraine, driven sideways, lost his balance. He went down unavoidably, still glued to the rifle. Though shaken by the fall, he got off two rounds dead into the muzzle flare.

Through the din of these shots he caught a rhythm of boot sound, the noise of this runner beating up from behind. Frantically rolling, he squirmed half around to squeeze trigger again.

The pound of boots quit and Caltraine, pushing worriedly up off the ground, thought he had got him till a racket of hooves made off in the timber. Listening to that diminishing thunder, he cursed, grimly turning to peer somewhat dubiously into the black where that ambusher had been, finally shaking his head.

He had his human share of curiosity but common sense told him to leave it alone. That guy could be dead or foxily waiting for Caltraine to walk into it.

He wouldn't know the man anyway. If it was someone that Flake had put on his trail there'd be nothing to tie the sheriff into this. That, he guessed, you could pretty well bank on.

Those fellows most probably had exceeded their orders. It simply didn't make sense that anyone sitting on top like this sheriff—if you could put any trust in what the girl said—would try a thing crazy as this to be rid of him.

Yet the more he pushed it around the less sure he became.

She'd said Flake would know she had talked to him. That talk in itself could account for their jumping him. They could have been told that if Caltraine tried for Wolftrap to drop him.

He thought of something else, an even stronger motivation. Wong's suggestion that Joe had picked the wrong friends tied in, he recokoned, with the four the girl said Flake had run off their range. It wasn't the sort of thing any sheriff would mix himself up in without being prepared to go all the way. And there was Joe, for example, shot down in the street with half the town looking on. This kind of thing inevitably brought the risk of somebody seeking to invoke higher authority. If Flake suspected Caltraine was a federal marshal he would stop at nothing to protect what he had going.

Caltraine went back to the mule and got into the saddle. His wound was beginning to make itself noticed. He felt the wet stickiness of cloth at each move; there was an ache in his ribs; his left side was afire.

He took stock of his position and could not see that he had much choice. Flake was playing for pretty high stakes. In control of the county law machinery, he had a damn good chance of stopping any stranger who elected to run. The girl had been right; his best bet was Wolftrap.

Climbing toward the pass, Caltraine's mind wasn't idle. He kept both eyes peeled, knowing whoever had torn off on that horse would be having second thoughts about reporting a failure. Dollars to doughnuts the son of a bitch would have another go at it.

Probing the tree thickened gloom at both sides of the road, Caltraine kept his rifle in clammy hands, ready to blast at the first hint of movement. The fire on his ribs seemed to grow with each jolt and he worried some too about the blood he was losing. But he didn't dare stop to see about it now.

He got through the pass without encountering anyone.

Angling down the far side, he spied the cliffs she had mentioned. They made a wide chalky line against the dark blur that off to the right flanked the gut of a canyon. He had to peer twice through the glimmer of starshine to locate the break masking the trail into Wolftrap. Even then he couldn't be sure the deeper dark he'd got his eyes on was anything more than a fold in the bluffs.

He was not too crazy about the look of this road. Narrower here, a dusty strip closely girt by black shapes of tall pines, one blind bend after another as it snaked about the convolutions of the main rock mass, in spots precariously held in place by built-up walls of unmortared stone overlooking sheer drops to the canyon floor. If that vanished horsebacker was back of one of these bends . . .

In this uncomforting thought Caltraine was half minded to get out of the saddle; if he hadn't been wounded he would probably have done so. But he hated the prospect of losing more blood.

Half down the grade, he moved off into timber but found the going too rough in that heavier black and returned to the road. He paused to hark a while before continuing his descent toward the floor. Hugging the bends, rifle constantly ready, he felt like a goddamn thief in the night.

There was no guarantee the man was ahead of him. There was a fair possibility he had cut in behind, slipping along like a breechclothed Indian, dogging his tracks till he could get a clear shot.

Despite the mixed notions rolling round through his head, Caltraine got down to the bottom of the road without having occasion to burn any powder.

Plain lucky, he guessed, and caught the first full breath

he had drawn in two hours. His eyes squinted at the bluffs perhaps a hundred yards off. Forming the northern wall of the canyon here, they went straight up, an almost sheer ninety feet. No chance getting a horse over that kind of rock.

He couldn't see from here the darker patch glimpsed above. Near as he could remember it was off someplace to the west of him. He recalled the girl advising that he approach the track into Wolftrap boldly but that ruckus back yonder did not make this too feasible.

He went forward with care, mind on the rider of that horse he'd heard running, scanning intently each dark blotch encountered. The canyon floor was festooned with shadows, prickly pear clumps, thorny huddles of cholla, fallen rock and mesquite. Any one of these in this light could have covered a crouching man.

Then abruptly he saw the black slot he was hunting, the crevice the girl had said would fetch him into Joe Ambruster's basin. Still going forward, he came onto a wash, cut in past times by the all-year creek that had gone underground before coming onto this range Flake had grabbed.

Caltraine moved up the wash toward the black gash in the cliffs, not hurrying his mount, every nerve coiled in caution.

The shot came without warning.

Untouched, he heard the sound of it roll across the canyon and break against rock. He pulled himself out of his muscle-locked freeze to throw back his head and yell, "Watch what you're doing!" at the black ramparts over him. "The girl sent—"

The rest was drowned out in a sudden rush of firing—not from the rimrocks this time but from out of the blackness off to the left.

He heard the burro fall gasping behind him and let go of the lead-rope as the mule, bit in teeth, flattened big ears in a ragged, ungainly bolt for the slot. The gun up above was thrown into the racket. Hooves barreled toward Caltraine's plunging mule. Flame leaped out of the swirling black night from ten feet away and Caltraine shot back at it, half emptying his carbine before the walls of the crevice shut everything out and kept him from knowing if this fire was effective.

He let the mule run, not knowing the temper of that man on the rimrocks. The passage twisted a little as they banged through the dark but not nearly enough to cut off flying bullets if that fellow back there was still able to sling them. He gourged the mule with his heels, trying to shake more speed out of him, and saw too late the heavy poles of a padlocked gate rushing toward him.

Caltraine was trying to lift the mule over it with the reins when they struck with a tremendous meaty impact. Caltraine—flung loose—went hurtling through space.

8

When he got back to the land of the quick the sun was at least four hours high and he was flat on his back in a barracks-like room that was crammed with cigarette smoke and scowling men.

No one had to advertise his status as a prisoner. Even without the stares he was getting the fact was self-evident in the absence of his hardware. "He's come out of it," one of them growled, and the others crowded nearer to peer, openly suspicious.

Four of them, Caltraine now discerned. There wasn't any sweetness in them, nor any suggestion they would hang together even in this matter of a stranger's presence.

A pimply faced kid with a black tangle of hair and an unstable look that was threaded with danger bent to peer closer, his tawny glance lighting up like a fire freshly fed. "What the hell we waitin' for? Let's get to work on him."

A leather faced man shoved the kid aside. His thick curling hair was the gray of cast iron and Caltraine could see he'd be a hard one to know with that tight, pressed-in mouth and eyes two shades colder than the winds off Antarctica. It didn't seem at all likely very much would escape them.

This man, lifting a boot to the bunk's bottom corner, propped elbow on knee and studied him some more. "You're new around here. How'd you stumble on this place?"

"The girl sent me out."

"She got a name?"

"The one that's been taking care of Joe's father."

"You talking about Terry Ambruster?"

Ignoring the skepticism, Caltraine replied, "She didn't give me her name. Just asked me to come out and help you boys keep Flake off that water."

Growls came from the others while the thin mouth tightened and the cold eyes stared without readable expression. The pimply faced kid cried, "He's lyin', Tuebelo! Terry wouldn't of—"

Tuebelo's stiffened hand chopped the boy's open mouth with a full-length swing that spun him stunned and yelling half across the room. "When I want your advice," Tuebelo said, "it'll be asked for." He brought his hard stare back to Caltraine's face. "That's your story?"

"It's the one I've been stuck with. There was some kind of guff about stopping outside with empty hands in plain sight and taking off my hat, but things warmed up before I got to that part of it. Not craving to share the fate of my burro, when those guns opened up the only thought I hung onto was to get me some cover."

"How'd she happen to latch onto you?"

"I got into a little trouble with your high and mighty sheriff."

The kid, over Tuebelo's shoulder, sneered. The other pair watched with blank faces while waiting on the gray haired man's decision.

Tuebelo said, "What kind of trouble?"

Caltraine rasped a grimy hand across his jaw. "Advised me to get myself a job. Real quick."

"The trouble man."

"We had a kind of a set-to over the girl."

The kid's mouth twisted. The other two exchanged indecipherable glances, the shorter one asking, "Where was Joe all this time?"

"Dead," Caltraine said, and told them about picking up the girl and what Flake had said in the privacy of his office. Without saying he'd been hired to boss this outfit he told most of the rest of it to explain his presence. Then he got around to asking, "What happened to my mule?"

The shorter man, whose name was Gurd Bedderman, replied. "You'll not thank us for this but we plain had to shoot him," adding, "Your friend with the rifle got clean away."

Then Tuebelo, straightening, remarked rather quietly, "Don't it seem a little odd, if you're telling the way it happened, the girl didn't warn you about that locked gate?" The kid broke out his hungry grin, crowding up close, to see things take a more pleasing turn.

Caltraine, watching, said reasonably, "Expect she figured I would follow instructions; she could hardly have reckoned there wasn't going to be time."

Tuebelo's studying gaze turned more darkly inscrutable. There was no way of telling what thoughts had clicked over behind those blank cheeks. "About Joe . . ." he said. "What triggered the action?"

The room seemed to be getting a little fuzzy round the edges and Caltraine, peering up at them, blinked. His head hurt almost as much as his side and he wondered how much that spill had taken out of him. Harassed by these distractions he was in poor shape to give a proper judgment but told as best he could what he had seen when he'd come out of Wong's store just before Joe had put on his run for the stage.

Tuebelo, when he was done, only nodded. But the fourth man took this opportunity to be heard from, saying, "Seems funny they got onto him this time. He's been in and out of that town often enough without nobody ever knowin' he was around."

Tuebelo shrugged. "Any pail can be took to the well too often."

"What did he go in for?" Caltraine asked, curious.

"Supplies," Bedderman said with a kind of nervous shiver. "We been gettin' low, brother, and I suppose he wanted to see his old man."

Caltraine could understand that. Joe would hardly have chanced touring the town himself no matter how short they were. He would have gotten the grub from his father, of course, or sent the girl in to buy it for him. He remembered how she'd slipped past on the porch, going down those steps to move into the street just before Joe had lunged away from that wall. He couldn't think if she'd had bundles or not.

He looked at Tuebelo again, found the man's stare still weighing him, not satisfied, but with some inner shining he couldn't quite put a finger on. It seemed almost as if the man were excited, but if this was so he kept it out of his voice. "We've patched you up," he told Caltraine, "the best we was able, but if you aim to be smart you'll stay in that bunk till them wounds heal over."

"How bad is it?"

"That place on your side won't give you no trouble but that cut on your head don't look good to me. You probably got a concussion. Man's lost as much blood as you have ain't got no business waltzin' around."

"I guess what you mean—"

"What I mean is you stay in that bed till I tell you different," Tuebelo said, and walked out of the room, the kid striding after him.

Bedderman, too, presently went out, leaving Caltraine alone with the fourth man. "What do we call you?" this one asked.

"Vic Walters."

The fellow nodded, a nondescript codger with a large Adam's apple and a chin that had missed its full share of bone. "Hobey Alred here," he mentioned, eyeing Caltraine curiously from under the tufts of oversized eyebrows. "How come you had all them shells in your pockets?"

Caltraine told his story of being jumped by Indians. "That gent at the Mercantile staked me to an outfit. I never was much of a shot with a rifle. Thought I'd better get in some practice."

Alred nodded. "Might save your life sometime. This here is hard country." He scratched himself and got up, saying with some slyness, "I never would of took you for a minin' man, Walters."

"Matter of fact, I'm what you might call a half-ass engineer," Caltraine explained, half turning over to get comfortable. "Work's been slow here of late. Thought I might as well try my hand at prospecting."

Alred grinned back at him. "Man never knows." He reached for the door. "I better get at my chores."

Left to himself, a vague uneasiness that had been trying to get through to him off and on ever since he had opened his eyes on this room sent Caltraine's hands abruptly down to his middle. The shock he got then almost shoved him bolt upright. He'd been completely undressed. But it wasn't the lack of his clothes that excited him half as much as the loss of his money belt.

9

He must have been out again because the next time he consciously took stock of his surroundings the room was dark. He seemed still to be alone. He was about to get up to have a look for his clothes when he caught a jumble of voices coming from outside, too low for him to pick out the words. With a grunt he lay back, trying to figure his next move.

There was no use working up a sweat about this. This outfit of Joe's had him over a barrel and, for the moment at least, there wasn't much he could do but bide his time. No clothes, no guns, no transportation and no money made the kind of odds no gambler would take without he had lost the biggest share of his think wheels. Somebody around here was being pretty shrewd and, in Caltraine's book, that had to be Tuebelo.

In the first consternation of discovering his loss Caltraine had reckoned the kid had got the bankroll. Now he ruled this out. It simply wasn't likely; a fellow knocked around as that kid had been by Tuebelo would not dare stand against him in a matter of such magnitude.

There'd been eighty thousand dollars in that belt they'd taken off him. Stood to reason Tuebelo had it.

Tuebelo's first intention, doubtless, had been aimed at immobilizing Caltraine, which was why they had taken his clothes and hardware. No one, they'd feel, who had all his buttons would be apt to light out with his ass bare.

They wanted him anchored till they made up their minds, till they found an opportunity to check out his story.

Still, the thing cut both ways.

Caltraine, pushing it around, could see how he might get *some*thing for that money. Viewed in the light of their own situation each of those four would be doing a pile of thinking. Tuebelo would know this. He'd not be able to trust any of them, down and out like they were, bottled up here with nothing but an unmarked grave and that money to think about. And the longer Tuebelo sat on it the more chance he took.

Caltraine grimly smiled. Get them fighting among themselves and he stood a slim chance to cut loose of this outfit. Their problems weren't his—nor that girl's ambition, either. He meant to get out on the first chance that offered.

The approach of booted feet caught at his notice and he tensed up, wondering what they'd be trying to pull now. It came over him suddenly that the girl herself might have tipped Flake off to Joe's presence there in town last night.

Hobey Alred came in, trailed by Tuebelo and gimpy Bedderman, the latter peering suspiciously about with the lamp he'd just lit lifted over his head. And Tuebelo, coming heavily to slouch against the next tier of bunks, folded his lips in a scowl to say grumpily, "What's been chewing on your apple, Walters?" Slaty eyes sharply searched as they prowled Caltraine's face.

"Just been thinking," he answered. "That Ambruster girl seemed almighty worried. By her tell Flake's some impatient to get his hooks on this pocket on account of that water, yet the first sight I get after waking up here is the four of you standing round waiting to pump me. With nobody watching, what's to stop that bunch from riding straight in and plain taking over?"

Tuebelo grinned. "There's just one way in. That slot you come through. One man with a rifle—"

"*I* got in."

"Yeah. Bedderman's shift. He couldn't seem to make his mind up. You got in all right." Tuebelo said with a chuckle, "When you fixing to take over?"

Caltraine frowned. "But when I came to, all four of you were in—"

"Coosie was up on the rimrocks that time," Alred said.

"Mean there's five of you here?"

"Five counting Coosie. He's out there on watch now."

"I understand from what the girl told me . . ."

"The girl or the sheriff?" said Tuebelo.

Caltraine's stare was heavily freighted. "She'll take care of your doubts when she gets here."

"When, and *if*."

"Considering the size of her investment you can bet she'll want to know what's happened. I wasn't sent out here to stay in a bed."

When Tuebelo continued to stare without comment Caltraine said on a harder note, "If this Coosie's up on the rimrocks now, where's the kid who was so interested in me? And I'd like to know, too, what's become of that bankroll I had in my belt?"

A silence shut down on them. Bedderman wheeled aside to set the lamp on a shelf with a visible scowl. Hobey Alred, flushing, confined his attention to unbroken appraisal of a crack in the flooring.

None of which noticeably appeared to bother Tuebelo. Through an amused slanch of grin he drawled coolly enough, "If you mean Johnnie Ruddabaugh he's off takin' care of your mule and that burro." He put away his grin to assume an air of sham concern. "Seems that bump on the head must of done you a sharper hurt than I figured." He wheeled a look at the other two. "You fellers noticed any money floatin' round?"

Alred's flush darkened. Gurd Bedderman made a non-committal grunt.

Tuebelo, shrugging, spread both hands. "You want to search our belongin's?"

Had Caltraine been sound at the moment it would have been a different story. Wishing wasn't going to butter any parsnips and whoever had it would certainly not have left it where any cursory search would pull the rug out from under him.

Glaring with disgust for the unthinking haste which had placed him at such sorry disadvantage Caltraine twisted over to ease his aching side. He heard the door slam behind Tuebelo's departing steps and the boots of somebody else presently clumping across the uncovered floor, then the creak of bunk ropes as the fellow sat down to get ready for bed.

Somebody let out a gusty sigh and with the lamp still lit the place settled into an uneasy quiet. "You reckon Joe really got planted?" Alred asked. Bedderman's grunt was the last thing heard before Caltraine dropped into a dream-harried sleep.

The supplies packed in by the kid, Johnnie Ruddabaugh, from Caltraine's dead burro would piece out the grub situation for another week or ten days, Tuebelo thought. After that, it appeared, one of the four would have to make the same trip which had eliminated Joe. No one rushed forward to volunteer but Tuebelo settled this by tagging the kid. When Ruddabaugh would have argued the matter the leather faced man chopped off protest with a hard, challenging stare.

Another night went by without sign of the girl.

By the following afternoon it had become pretty obvious, to Caltraine at least, if he were going to get out of this it would have to be through some move of his own. He'd been up several times to relieve calls of nature and the last time, this morning, he'd gone out to the three-holer under Bedderman's nervous care without the usual giddiness. But to get back his strength he needed to be up and around and Tuebelo—until now, anyway—had made this impossible.

In the afternoon, right after grubpile, all four of them had gone off someplace on horseback, leaving Coosie to his pots and pans with instructions to keep a sharp eye on "our guest."

The cook, an old stove-up puncher, must have been all of forty, and was potbellied and crotchety. He seldom opened his mouth without he was spoken to, as short on wind as a dismantled mill and about as friendly as a prodded snake.

After trying several times to engage him in conversation Caltraine, still abed, said, "Coosie, I believe you and I could do a mite of business."

When this remark shared the fate of previous overtures Caltraine, throwing back the cotton blanket, sat up and swung both feet to the floor. Coosie's reaction was sharp and sudden. He spun from his tasks with a leveled six-shooter. "Get back in that bunk!"

Caltraine stayed where he was. "You don't look like a fool," he said quietly. "You want to spend all the rest of your life over a cookstove?"

Coosie's knuckles showed white round the gun. "I'm not tellin' you twice—git under that cover!"

10

Caltraine's mind held no doubt the man meant it but he realized, too, that for every gain something had to be risked. You could still be scared and bust a gut trying. Glance locked with Coosie's, Caltraine stayed where he was.

Cook's finger tightened. The hammer started its short rise from the breech. The cylinder moved a whispered click to the left while Caltraine, rigid almost as a spring coiled to snapping, tried to gauge the changing lights in the cook's eyes.

Sweat made a shine across the man's upper lip. Caltraine said meagerly, "Ever had your mitts on a thousand dollar banknote?"

The hammer stood like the lifted tail of a vinegar-roon while the cook tried to tear his mind from those words.

Caltraine, tautly smiling, knew it could go either way. "I can fix it so you can get out of here with one if you're willing to make it worth my while."

The cook continued cantankerously to stare, suspicion

still bright, but he appeared willing to leave the door a little open.

He took the weight off one leg and put it on the other. "Where you figurin' to find that kinda money?"

"I can get it when you're ready to do business," Caltraine said.

Ingrained caution made the man stare some more. His hungry look jittered around the room. "An' if I said I was ready?"

"You could be out of this place inside of ten minutes."

"With the money?"

"With the money."

"An' what about Tuebelo?" Coosie asked with a sneer.

"Put a gun in my fist and I'll take care of Tuebelo."

"Yeah. That figures. An' the rest of us, too."

"All right. Forget about the gun. Just fetch my clothes and we'll call it a deal," Caltraine said.

Coosie finally put up his pistol, eyes searching Caltraine as though he still couldn't believe it. "That's all I got to do? Just fetch your duds an' you'll hand over the dinero?"

"That's right."

"When do I get paid?"

"Soon's I get dressed."

The cook pulled at his nose. "Where the hell you gonna get it?"

"If I told you that you wouldn't need to help, would you?"

"Goddamn!" Coosie said. "Don't make sense you'd cough up a thousand just to get into your goddamn clothes!"

"Makes sense to me."

The man said bitterly, "I don't believe you've got a thin dime. We went through your stuff with a fine tooth comb —leastways Tuebelo did after that belt showed up."

"I'll bet," Caltraine chuckled. He scratched at his chest through the moth-eaten blanket and said, "No gambling man puts all his eggs in one basket. If his luck turns sour he wants a stake to come back on.''

"Stay put," Coosie growled. "I'll be right back," and he went into the yard, pulling the door shut behind him.

Caltraine wasted no time. He had the cover thrown back before the cook had got the door shut, levering himself shakily out of the bunk.

The door was off to one side. When the door stood open this part of the room was pretty much screened. He picked up several things he'd had his eye on, thrust them onto the bunk and pulled the blanket over them. The result at first glance was a recumbent man; he didn't aim for the cook to have more than one look.

Feeling weak as a kitten, he crossed to the stove. The cast iron skillet weighed as much as a horse to him after the liquid diet this bunch had been feeding him. Recrossing the room with it, he took up a stance next to the door.

His heart thumped like an excited rabbit. He could feel sweat cracking through the pores of his skin. He would never get out of here without a gun—that it might cost his life was a chance he had to take.

Gauging chances was something he'd been accustomed to doing ever since he'd quit home. But Caltraine knew better than to put any trust in a man staying bought. There was the rest of them, too.

No matter how far he got in this attempt there was still Tuebelo to be reckoned with, and in his present condition nothing short of a gun was like to take him past that one.

The sound of boots outside reached him. He stepped forward a half pace away from the wall, arming himself with enough room to swing, and lifted the skillet.

The boots came on across a clatter of shale, pausing outside as fingers jiggled the latch. Caltraine took a deep breath and the door was shoved open.

He heard the boots stop and all his thinking stopped with them.

"Walters?"

If Coosie's suspicions kept him rooted, not letting him budge without reassurance—or if he ducked back instead of coming on in—all hopes in this sequence would be washed down the drain.

Without breath Caltraine waited.

"Walters!"

Fright and anger jumped cook's voice to a snarl. Caltraine heard the snick of a gun leaving leather. In a half crouch, the man dived past the door's edge and Caltraine, with all the strength in him, brought down the iron skillet.

With a muffled whoom of sound, the blow flattened cook's hat against the top of his skull and drove him floorward like a bursting sack to sprawl spread-eagled and desperately striving with one clawing hand to reach that dropped gun.

Caltraine's bare foot sent the pistol skittering. He cursed with the pain of it and flung himself forward on a whistle of breath to deal the man another round of the same. It was a first-class notion but a little too late. While the skillet was still on its upward arc, Tuebelo's voice shouted: *"Hold it!"*

Caltraine froze, all his hopes crashing round him.

"Back off," Tuebelo said from the doorway. Caltraine straightened. Had he not been so weak he might have tried throwing the skillet, but he was too near collapse to have any faith in his present abilities.

He stepped back groggily and Tuebelo said, "Let go of it, man. Let go of it."

What else was there left?

Caltraine dropped his weapon. Coosie got up, holding onto his head, enough venom in his stare to wilt an oak post. Tuebelo said, "Get into them duds," and kicked the dropped clothes against Caltraine's wobbly legs.

When their prisoner was dressed, Tuebelo told him to

get back on the bunk. Coosie stepped over to pick up his six-shooter, looking about half minded to use it.

Tuebelo said, "Suppose you could rope me out a fresh bronc and saddle one for this feller without makin' a botch of it?"

Coosie, glaring, slammed the gun in his holster and clomped through the door mad enough to chew nails.

Caltraine hadn't figured to open his mouth but as the silence piled up under Tuebelo's stare he finally said, "What was that about horses?"

"You wanted out, didn't you? I'm fixin' to take you."

11

Staring hotly, Caltraine considered the man's twisted features. Nobody had to spell it out for him. If he rode from this place with that cold jawed customer it could well be the last anyone ever saw of him.

"Aren't you getting kind of arbitrary, friend?"

"You're goin'. You'll go if I have to have you roped to the saddle. I got too much already sunk into this to have it loused up by any star dodgin' drifter."

Notions passed through Caltraine's mind like a stampede of longhorns, but only a fool would have hoped to get by that arm-folded bastard standing off against the wall.

"Nothing ventured, nothing lost," Tuebelo said with a piece of a grin. "Out on the trail you might get lucky. You try somethin' here, all you'll get is a bullet."

Caltraine was no stranger to threatening dilemmas, but always before he'd glimpsed a possible out—had been in shape anyway to take a whack at providing one. It wasn't only his rifle-creased side that stood in his way. Three days and nights on a gruel of broths, on top of lost blood and being flat on his back weren't quite the odds to hold out much hope for attempted exertions.

He heard a clatter of hooves and this, near as anything, knocked over the last prop of his incipient rebellion. Whatever chance there was now was plainly out of his reach. Blowing out his held breath in a snort of disgust, he slumped down on the blanket as the hooves stopped outside.

Saddle leather creaked. Spurs scraped the ground and Coosie stepped in with Bedderman trailing. "All right," grunted Tuebelo. "On your feet, Walters." He came away from the wall. "Let's get this over with."

Caltraine, if he hadn't much choice before, had considerable less with three of them facing him, guns on hips. Only Bedderman, plainly victim of his own timidity, showed any sign of being dubious about this. His kind weren't made of the stuff to take a sharp stand on anything.

Caltraine quit the bunk and got into the boots which had been kicked to the side of it. Coosie went out and Bedderman, appearing about to open his mouth, eyed Tuebelo again and, seeming more disgruntled, tramped after the cook without letting what was bothering him get into words.

Caltraine, sighing, straightened.

Taking Caltraine's pistol from inside his shirt, Tuebelo tossed it across with a mocking nod. "I like to see a man comfortable. After you, bucko."

There were times when he'd felt like he might be here forever, as though this place might turn out to be the end of his rope. The irony of Tuebelo tossing him a weapon which was sure to have been emptied seemed like unnecessarily rubbing his nose in it. Caltraine shoved the gun brusquely into his belt. "Any idea what Joe was doing in town?"

"Understand he told cook he was goin' after supplies. Maybe he figured to fetch 'em back in his pockets, taking just the one horse. . . . My guess is he went in to make a deal."

"You mean . . . sell out the rest of you?"

"Wouldn't be the first batch of friends sold down the river. Only Flake wasn't buying. No skin off your nose either way," he said gruffly, and motioned toward the door.

Crossing in front of him, Caltraine stepped out and saw, somewhat startled, what had been disquieting Bedderman.

The girl was there astride a dun horse, with a rifle across her lap, her stare locking Tuebelo into his tracks.

"Going someplace?"

A darkness came up under Tuebelo's collar, though he said cool enough, "Now that Walters is healed I was fixin' to show—"

She punched a look at Caltraine. "You been hurt?"

He shrugged it off, skewered by the unwinking stares of the others. "Guess you were right about Flake and that talk. Put a couple of his two-legged dogs on my trail. One of them got lucky, burned my ribs with a Winchester."

He made it appear hardly worth discussing, knowing all the while how vulnerable he was, ringed by this group with nothing in his belt but an unloaded pistol. There was no way he could warn the girl without precipitating trouble he was in no shape to meet.

Her glance passed around. Perhaps she smelled something queer in this fixity of stillness. Looking back to Tuebelo, she said, "I guess Walters told you about Joe, didn't he?"

Tuebelo tipped his head half an inch. The other pair, rooted, stood like sentries at either side of her, waiting for Tuebelo to give them a cue. She said, "I think he was running. He was trying to get on the stage when they killed him."

"What did he tell you?"

"I don't know what he told his father—he must have slipped in while I was down at Wong's place. I didn't get to talk with him. He was making for the stage when I came out of the Mercantile. I yelled, started running. One of the stage horses knocked me down. . . . Half the town saw it."

Bedderman licked at his lips but stayed silent. Tuebelo watched her without expression. The horse fiddled under her and backed five steps that put all four of them in front where she could see them. Something changed in her eyes. "Where's Alred and Johnnie Ruddabaugh?"

Tuebelo said, "Kid's up on the rim. I sent Alred—"

"And who gave you leave to send anyone anywhere?" There was a flatness of challenge that tightened the corners of her lips.

The man's jawline hardened. "You disputin' Joe's judgment?"

She met his stare with the firmness of rock. "I'd have to know first of all that this *was* Joe's judgment. I'll not bandy words with you. Every manjack in Wolftrap knows Joe intended this spread to come to me if anything happened to him."

"Looks like he changed his mind." Tuebelo smiled. "You just got through sayin' Joe didn't speak to you—"

"What's that have to do with it?" she said with her chin up. "We had our understanding."

At the edge of his patience, Tuebelo said, "Maybe he decided he was puttin' too much trust in you. He wanted this place kept out of Flake's hands. He'd have to be pretty damn soft in the head to imagine any woman would be able to do that!"

What the white-cheeked girl had in mind to say was left unspoken. Someone else spoke before she could start it, and the words he put flatly across that taut silence left no doubt at all about his intentions. "First gent to reach is goin' to wake in Boot Hill. Unlatch that artillery, Tuebelo, or both of them arms gets knocked off at the elbow."

12

The stillness stretched till Tuebelo finally put a hand to his middle and, still without turning, unbuckled his gun belt. The dark leather, metal weighted, whispered down one leg to strike the ground with a plop closely echoed by the hysterical cry forced by tension from Bedderman's throat.

"Good work!" Terry Ambruster said with satisfaction. Behind Caltraine the voice, grown pushy, bade Bedderman step over and secure Tuebelo's armament. "And watch it because the first wrong move is like to set this piece to kickin'," he was told.

Bedderman was cautious. When he had the belt in hand, he was instructed: "Just hand it up to Miz' Terry there—careful. Now step over by Coosie and the two of you git your backs up again' them corral poles."

It left Caltraine and Tuebelo midway between the corral and the shack's open door. It was taking a foolhardy chance, Caltraine couldn't help thinking, to be leaving that pair with loaded guns on their hips—particularly Coosie, who had something to prove.

Or was that what was aimed at? Some fool left loose to spin and spark in this powderkeg of weltering emotions.

Big roweled spurs moved nearer behind and he tensed, eyeing Tuebelo warily. Whether he was following Joe's orders or out to doublecross him, Tuebelo wasn't built to take reverses quietly. There was a deadly smoldering strength at work here, calculated to see through to bitterest finish whatever he tackled.

Tuebelo was another who had something to prove.

In common with the rest he'd been ousted by Flake, but unlike them he meant to do something about it. It was deep in his eyes, in that tight folded mouth—his whole bearing. He'd move heaven and earth to get back at Ben Flake. Caltraine felt the danger that was in him, and worried.

The spur sound cut left and Johnnie Ruddabaugh stepped into plain sight beyond Tuebelo's shoulder. Although puffed by Terry's praise he was aware enough of Tuebelo's character to keep well clear of him even with that pistol sticking out of his fist.

Caltraine knew then there was going to be trouble.

This unstable kid with his hunger for notice hadn't the experience nor savvy to control for very long a man with the undoubted talents of Tuebelo. Flushed with his easy triumph, Ruddabaugh seemed blind to the venom in Coosie's hot glance as he preened before the girl like some patted terrier. He turned to grin into Tuebelo's face. "Why'n't you try takin' a poke at me now?"

Tuebelo's stare showed nothing but Coosie, quick to seize opportunity, grabbed for his shooter and the gun half out when the kid, still grinning, came around like a cat, flame leaping out of the snout of his pistol.

Cook's mouth stretched wide. His legs doubled under him. He fell on his face, both hands clutched to his middle.

Bedderman's eyes almost rolled off his cheekbones. He

began to shake like a dog in a blue norther. His face turned green and he was violently sick.

"You want to try something now?" the kid said to Tuebelo.

The man had his hands in plain sight, face expressionless. It was plain to Caltraine he was not much surprised. "No, but your point couldn't've been made without killing that damn bungler," Tuebelo said.

"Thought maybe you might stand in need of an example."

Caltraine saw the girl shudder, but she didn't get sick as Bedderman had done. Nor forget the unfinished business between herself and Tuebelo. The barrel of her rifle rested coldly in line with his belt buckle. Johnnie, noticing the tightness of her expression, called up his cracked laugh.

"You don't have to worry none about *him*, missy." The boy showed his teeth in callow contempt and spat at Tuebelo's boots, laughing again when the man ignored him. "He's anybody's dog that'll whistle . . . ain't you, Rover? Come on now, show the nice lady how you put up your paws."

Caltraine thought Tuebelo was much too quiet, going along with it whimsically, putting up his arms. If the man ever got those big hands on Johnnie there'd be one sharp crunch and that would be the end of him.

The kid couldn't see it. His overweening pride was this ability with a pistol. He couldn't seem to envisage a time he might be without it. "You see?" he said from his ten feet of importance. "Show his kind who's the boss and they'll jump when you tell them—ain't that so, Bedderman?"

The short, frightened man nodded nervously, his normally florid features looking pasty as wet wood ash.

The kid laughed again with a kind of exultation until Terry Ambruster said quietly, "But you're not going to be the boss of Wolftrap, Johnnie."

The kid stared, stunned, with his jaw hanging open.

With a sigh, Caltraine braced himself. He had known all the while he would probably be faced with this. She had no way of knowing the gun he wore was empty.

"The job's already filled," she told Ruddabaugh gently.

But he didn't want gentleness. He wanted to be top dog in this layout of misfits, and the enormity of her decision spread a flush across his cheeks. Anger shook the arm he whipped to point at Tuebelo. "You think you kin trust that sonofabitch? You better know he's been—"

Tuebelo said, using his voice like a club, "Button your lip, boy."

Ruddabaugh, rooted, let the arm slowly drop. He'd been too long under the man's domination to throw off at once the habit of surly obedience which, at least to this point, must have held him in thrall.

His eyes were like holes burnt in a bedsheet. He drew a hand across his mouth, hotly glaring, and into that silence the girl coolly spoke.

"I'm not talking about him. The man I sent up here, Walters, will be responsible hereafter for keeping Chainlink riders away from Wolftrap water."

Ruddabaugh, again shocked, flung her an affronted, disbelieving stare. Tuebelo stayed in his tracks, thinly smiling. The girl said firmly, "He'll take care of my interests—"

"That's a helluva thing," cried Ruddabaugh, furious. "Settin' some gunhandy stranger ahead of the outfit your brother put together! By God, I won't work for—"

"You will if you value my friendship."

Frustrated and sulking, he looked more like the overgrown kid he was than the calculating killer he'd just shown himself to be. His long rumpled hair hung across his bitter stare and Caltraine thought the pout on his mouth wasn't going to be removed by any offer of friendship.

Peering up at her obliquely, waving the gun in his fist, Ruddabaugh said meanly, "What's he figure to git outa this, you're so sure you kin trust him?"

"It seems reasonable as part owner his wants will coincide with mine."

13

Surprise firmed the set of Caltraine's features, but he could see this news was pouring no oil on Ruddabaugh's temper.

"Jesus Christ!" the boy cried while Tuebelo chuckled in sardonic amusement. "What do you find that's so goddamn funny!" Ruddabaugh muttered at him.

Tuebelo considered, grin still lurking at the edges of his eyes. "Ain't it funny to you that a out-at-knees drifter comes out of the brush to buy into this spread right under the nose of a guy just done tellin' him to either get lost or try duckin' blue whistlers? A badge that's just planted the spread's rightful owner?"

The girl said, "He didn't buy into it. I'm *giving* him his half—"

"Then more fool you," Tuebelo said, twisting his look and one shoulder around. "Any way you cut it, tying up with a bank robber won't buy you nothing but a wagonload of grief."

Bitting her lip, the girl's eyes raked Caltraine. "Who says he's a bank robber?"

Tuebelo's gray look showed its edge of contempt. "What else would he be with a money belt strapped under them kinda duds an' by God stuffed with eighty thousan' dollars?"

Reaching inside his shirt with a fine scorn for Ruddabaugh, he dragged out the belt and flung it, bulging, beneath the dun's shifting hooves. "Try countin' it yourself. You think maybe he shook some damn bush to get that?"

The doubts showed plain through Terry's questioning look. She stopped the horse's fiddling with tightened rein, still regarding Caltraine in a darkening appraisal. He could have told her the truth but it wasn't his intention to put new weapons in their hands. The girl, for her own reasons, might have let it ride but how far could one trust that unstable kid?

Trying to laugh it off, Caltraine said without humor, "If you're bound to swallow that kind of hogwash you'd better *habla* with the sheriff. He might feel it worth his while to comb through some of those dodgers folks send him."

Ignoring the kid's shooter and Tuebelo's scrutiny, he put a hand on the dun and, half twisting under him, picked up the scuffed belt and fastened it round him. He caught Tuebelo's stare. "Kind of reckoned when I missed this you'd be hunting greener pastures."

"I'm not in any hurry," he said equably, and looked at Terry. "Sure you want this hombre to hang on here as rep?"

It was clear he had put the girl in two minds about it. She peered from one to the other with a deepening frown but finally nodded, saying, "I . . . guess so."

"In that case you won't need me," Tuebelo said.

"Me, neither," the boy growled, ramming his pistol

back into its leather with a fierce sort of glower. "I'm not takin' orders from no johnny-come-lately—"

"You'll take them and you'll damn sure obey them. And that goes double for Tuebelo. Nobody's quitting this outfit," Caltraine said. He left it there flatly and waited for trouble.

The kid flushed and squirmed, wheeled to eye the girl accusingly. She didn't speak and Tuebelo shrugged. Caltraine, measuring the three steps between them, told Bedderman, "Give him back his smokepole."

Tuebelo caught the weighted belt the man tossed him and coolly flipped it about his waist.

This whole deal was getting just a little mite iffy.

It was hard to see exactly what Tuebelo was up to. He was obviously working for his own best interests but where he might figure these to lie at the moment appeared some obscure.

Whether he was fixing to team up with Flake or merely endeavoring to confuse the issue, his surprise production of the money belt was certainly not calculated to benefit Caltraine.

Caltraine, anyway, was bound by this assumption. Which was why—dangerously countering—he'd seen fit to re-arm the man. Telling the girl he'd been a prisoner here and that Tuebelo had been contemplating dropping him into some gulch wasn't like to help any.

He had to try to put the boot on the other foot a while, open up some doubts for Tuebelo to chew on.

The risk was in the realities. The girl, the kid and Bedderman, observing him heeled, had to suppose him armed. But Tuebelo—having personally seen to it—would know Caltraine's pistol was without any loads to back up his demands and therefore could, if it suited him, ignore them. He could, in fact, gun Caltraine down and go on roughshod with whatever his scheme was. Caltraine could only hope that the return of his weapon might disquiet the man enough to keep him tractable, for at least as long as the girl was around.

"Well, *boss*," Tuebelo said, mealymouthed, "what are your orders?"

"The kid better go relieve Alred."

Ruddabaugh, darkening, might have put up an argument had not Tuebelo's words stopped him. "You heard the man, boy—what the hell are you waitin' on?"

Flinging out his arms, blackly scowling, Ruddabaugh took off to go catch up his horse. But Terry Ambruster, puzzled, spoke, peering at Tuebelo. "Didn't you tell me you'd sent Alred—"

"Damn!" growled the straw boss, taken aback and looking properly disgruntled. "I mighty sure did—sent him to Lochiel to pick up supplies. I plumb forgot about that."

"So there's no one been watching that slot," Caltraine said without expression.

"Well . . . for mebbe half an hour. Flake's bunch wouldn't know that."

"They might, before night if Alred decided to turn up at Pine Knob instead of Lochiel," Caltraine said.

"Now why would Hobey do a thing like that? Man would have to be a plumb idiot after what happened to Joe to go pushin' his luck right into Flake's pocket."

Caltraine let it go. If for any reason Pine Knob was where the man had been sent Tuebelo certainly wasn't going to admit it. "You were going to show me over this spread today, weren't you?" he said on a different tack.

It was Tuebelo's excuse when they'd come out of the shack. Before he could think up another, the girl said, "I'll ride along. Give me a chance to see what shape the stock is in."

Tuebelo did not display much enthusiasm. Since he reluctantly agreed to go along with this nuisance, Caltraine tended to think Tuebelo might still have a use for the girl's good opinion.

This straw boss, Caltraine was impelled to acknowledge, looked considerably more than just a bullypuss foreman. A burgeoning ambition burned behind that crusty stare and possibly other things not as readily apparent. "Go saddle a couple of broncs," he told Bedderman. Then, grinning, looking at no one especially, "Just imagine Flake's face when somebody tells him about the new range boss we've got here at Wolftrap."

When nobody laughed he said, "Well, let's get at it," and stepped over to the door to pick up his rifle.

14

As they rode, Caltraine, turning over what he'd seen, wondered what if anything was between this girl and Ruddabaugh. The kid, when he'd put that gun on Tuebelo, must have had some reason for thinking she would stand behind him. He had seemed downright shocked when she'd named Caltraine boss, had looked in fact like a man double-crossed. This was something he had better remember.

At the first opportunity he intended to make tracks. Tuebelo's grinning allusion to Flake had hit the nail right on the head. The sheriff would know, from the man who'd put that burn across his ribs, that Caltraine now was holed up at Wolftrap. When he found out Caltraine was now boss, Flake was uncommonly likely to throw everything he'd got at them. Caltraine didn't aim to be around when disaster struck.

While he couldn't think too highly of Ambruster's judgment, one thing he had to concede in Joe's favor. The man had had the wit to mount his outfit handsomely. These were first-rate horses under them, not only sure-footed but with plenty of bottom. The cattle Caltraine saw did not come up to this high mark, being a pretty motley lot. Tuebelo estimated the basin carried about a hundred mother cows, but even as grade critters they weren't anything a man would write home about. They were in good flesh—it was the most you could say for them.

"Where'd he get the bulls for this bunch?"

"We got a couple fiesty longhorn runts," Tuebelo said. "Mostly he depended on Flake's and Rutherford's Herefords till he got forced off the open range."

"And when did that happen?"

"When Flake closed me out and, along with the others run off their spreads, I threw in with Joe. About six months ago."

"Joe had the use of some ten miles of browse southeast of this place until the sheriff decided to freeze him out," Terry Ambruster added.

Caltraine was making good use of his eyes, not giving too much notice to the gab. North of this point was a line of chalky bluffs some three miles away. "What's back of those?" he asked Tuebelo, pointing.

"Alkali flats an' a pile of damn boulders—not that it makes any difference. You couldn't get cows through if it was knee-high in grama."

"Let's take a look."

Tuebelo shrugged. "You got somethin' in mind?" he asked, looking thoughtful as the horses took them up the steepening grade through a series of benches grown to cat-claw and buckbrush. Where rocks outcropped from the thin sandy soil they were buff colored, chalky, akin to caliche.

Caltraine seemed just a mite thoughtful, too. "Just curious to see where this goes," he replied, but his roving glance explored every detail, the whole lay of these gray tangled hills engraving itself on his memory.

"I could of told you," Tuebelo said with a snort. "It don't go nowhere. If a man could get through he'd probably wind up at Ruby or maybe Oro Blanco, but the far side's all cliffs. Can't get a horse over them."

When they finally rimmed out, all the animals panting, Caltraine could see for himself no horse was going to get past these drops. Not even a goat would tackle such sheer rock faces.

The girl said, as her eyes embraced the wild view, "Isn't it beautiful?"

"Quite a sight," Caltraine grunted, scarcely thinking about it. Mostly, at the moment, his thoughts were of Hobey Alred. The man like as not would return with supplies but Caltraine could not believe these were the whole or prime reason for his absence.

Tuebelo reined his horse about. "Maybe we ought to be gettin' back. No telling what that crazy kid'll be up to."

"You ever notice any cows coming this high up?" Caltraine asked, following, with the girl in between them.

"Why would they quit grass to nibble on this stuff? Ain't seen no droppin's around here, have you?"

Instead of pursuing the matter, Caltraine asked, "Where does that creek come into Wolftrap?"

Tuebelo waved a hand toward the west. "Off thataway."

Caltraine let ten minutes slide by while the horses twisted through a jumbled chaos of rocks and brush. "Any way Ben Flake could get at that water before we get hold of it?"

"Not a chance. Spring fed. Starts right here—comes up out of—"

"Let's take a look at it."

Tuebelo stopped, twisted round and slanched a look at the girl. She passed it along with the edge of a frown, not quite as impatient but certainly wondering. "Haven't you had enough riding for one day?'' She tucked in a strand of her chestnut hair. ''Are you always this curious?''

''Sometimes it pays. If I'm going to be responsible for this operation seems like I'd ought to know all there is to know about it.''

The girl studied him, then motioned to Tuebelo. ''Go ahead,'' she sighed. ''Might be a good idea if we all took a look at it.''

Half an hour later they were out of the bluffs swinging west just below them, through greasewood and cholla. There was grass showing here but it was old and yellow, too far from the water to show any green.

No one broke the riding silence until, cresting a ridge, the creek's course was picked out by an irregular growth of cottonwood and willow changing off farther up to a jungle of rocks and bean-hung mesquites. The girl said, ''How far up do we have to go?''

Tuebelo grunted. ''Coupla miles more or less. All you'll see is a passle of springs bubbling out of the rocks.'' He looked pretty disgusted. ''I could find better things to—''

''Fair enough,'' Caltraine said. ''If there's chores to be done don't let us keep you. I expect I can find 'em from here.''

Tuebelo scowled. ''No,'' the girl said. ''We'll all go. There's not much point in turning back now.''

Caltraine looked at them quizzically. Distrust flowed around like a current of air. The girl didn't trust Tuebelo out of her sight and the straw boss's look said he didn't trust either of them without he could see them. Without further words he put his horse to higher ground.

The ascent was more gradual through this stretch of hills. There was brush but not as much of it. The creek cooed and gurgled and birds chirped all around. Where the pitch of the ground began presently to stiffen, Caltraine, dropping out of line, cut over through the tangle to have a closer look at the stream itself. Here, running swiftly, it varied from one to two feet deep and, just this side of it, there were horse tracks. Fresh. These quickly caught his interest.

Before he was able to give them close scrutiny, approaching hooves and the swish of thorned branches wheeled him around to nudge his mount into motion just as Tuebelo broke into sight. "Just giving my horse a drink," Caltraine said, pushing on through to rejoin the girl, Tuebelo darkly riding in his wake.

There was something about his tight and closed face that warned Caltraine there was more to those tracks than met the eye. It did not seem farfetched to suppose they were Alred's, the hand he'd been told had been sent to Lochiel to pick up more grub.

Well. . . . Grub, like enough, could be purchased at Ruby.

15

For the rest of the climb Caltraine rode immersed in his thoughts. Lochiel was south, squatted alongside the Mexican border, and if that was where Alred had truly been sent what was he doing coming west through this hodgepodge of bleached and suncracked boulders?

Or was it someone else who had left those tracks?

Not likely, Caltraine concluded. No one else was left unaccounted for. Nor could he put much credence in the possibility that some hireling of Flake, or other outsider, had managed to slip in during the gunplay this morning. What outsider would bother climbing these hills? And to what purpose?

To spy and report on them? What could they learn that Flake didn't already know? The size of Joe's herd? How many guns he could count on? The disproportionate risk to whoever undertook it put this assumption at such long odds no gambler would touch it.

It had to be Alred who had put down those tracks; this opened up prospects that needed exploring. Either Tuebelo was out to take over Wolftrap or had well in hand some blacker piece of treachery . . . unless Alred himself had an iron in the fire.

Caltraine, thinking about this, called up a picture of a cat's narrow chin and feral green eyes blinking sleepily from under the springy tufts of Alred's hooded brows.

When they came to the source of Wolftrap's water high up on a bench overlooking the basin there was, as Tuebelo had prophesied, little to remark upon. Seven springs in all, bubbling up through faults in a formation more generally resembling limestone than any other substance Caltraine could put his mind to. There were no fresh horse tracks here.

Caltraine would have liked to have gone a bit farther just to make sure there was no way out from this side; but when Tuebelo said, "You satisfied now?" he did not think it prudent to call the man's attention to the direction his notions were beginning to fasten on.

He grunted, looking out across the heady sweep of panorama that ended in the dark upthrust of high-piled rock guarding Wolftrap's huddle of barely visible head-quarters. "Reckon so," he answered. Then, to give the man some other knot to chew on, he asked, "How long would you say it might take a man in a hurry to get up here from that slot?"

"You don't have to worry about that," the straw boss growled. "Ain't nobody gittin' through that slot without I say so."

Caltraine and the girl swapped speculative glances as the man turned away to step into his saddle. But the girl couldn't leave well enough alone. She was impelled to say dryly, "Seems to me you're forgetting something."

Tuebello's narrowing stare came around. "Like what?"

"Like what happened to Joe." Her chin firmed aggressively. "Like this spread has changed hands." There was frost in her smile. "Vic Walters is bossing this outfit now.

He'll be the one to say who'll come and who will go around here—remember?''

That was handing it to him straight off the platter, cold turkey style, and it was palpably evident the man didn't like it. In the coalescing flash of his tightening stare all Tuebelo's intolerance of petticoats showed; then he smoothed out his face in a parched grin that made him look like a snake getting ready to strike. But he had hold of himself enough to say, "Expect I can manage to keep that in mind." He jerked them a nod and reached again for the horn.

Caltraine hated to prod the man further but a showdown postponed could be even more unfavorable. Besides, he had a theory to test and this seemed as good a time as he would likely be handed. So he said, "You go on. We'll be along later."

Tuebelo stiffened, then got into his saddle. "Right," he grunted, and rode off downhill without another glance, even though he was armed and knew Caltraine wasn't.

So what could you make of that? Unless it was the girl which had turned him so cagey.

Considering this, Caltraine found himself more mixed up than ever. Why would Tuebelo be afraid of Joe's stepsister? If it had been in his head to take over this outfit you wouldn't hardly think he'd let a girl scare him off.

Caltraine's mind doubled back to the Pine Knob sheriff, the arrogant Flake who had acted in town as though the girl was his property, but he couldn't think that would cut much ice with Tuebelo. If anything wouldn't it be more likely to flush him into some kind of demonstration? Some open flatfooted violence to prove the contempt that burned so fierce behind that smoldering stare?

Terry Ambruster said, "Looks like our friend's got you fighting your hat. He's not hard to get to know when you understand his background. He's had a lot of hard luck and he's an ambitious man. He'd make two of Joe and everybody knows it. But Joe made a stand where Tuebelo wasn't able to, so he had to end up doing the next best thing. Warned off this range, he threw in with Joe and Joe decided to hole up in Wolftrap.''

She pushed back her hair. ''I think from the first he had his eye on this place—it could be what drove Joe into town that night. I think Joe knew the man was too tough to handle. He was half the reason I sent you . . . to keep Tuebelo from freezing me out. He's a lot like Flake when it comes to ambition.''

She shook her head somberly. ''Two years ago, before Flake was sheriff, Tuebelo owned a real up and coming outfit. Outwardly, at least, those two were friends seen everywhere together. Then Flake got himself elected sheriff. . . .''

Her eyes took on a faraway look. ''You might not think it, but Flake, when it suits him, can exert a lot of charm. Those days the both of them were courting the same girl . . . young widow she was with a nice piece of grass.

''I always figured Tuebelo had the inside track, but he couldn't believe it. And then one night he played into Flake's hands.''

''What happened?''

''Tuebelo killed her.''

Caltraine stared. ''He killed a *woman*?''

Terry nodded, a little more color creeping into her cheeks. ''They'd been taking turns calling. It was Flake's turn that night but Tuebelo showed up. I think he found them in bed, but Flake is the only one that's said what happened and of course he didn't tell it quite like that.

''At the inquest he said he'd just stepped up on the porch when a shot rang out and he saw Tuebelo taking off through a window. Says he yelled for him to stop, threw a cautioning shot after him. Then he rushed inside to find the girl in her bed with blood all over and a bullet in her chest. He said she died in his arms, Tuebelo's name on her lips.''

Caltraine, with their eyes locked, said, ''Of course he went after him.''

Terry's head tipped a nod. ''Flake went out to Tuebelo's ranch but the man wasn't there. He swore in a posse and combed the hills but Tuebelo by that time had got into Wolftrap. Been holed up here ever since.''

It figured, Caltraine thought. It might even, in a way, explain Tuebelo's reluctance to involve another woman . . . particularly if he'd been jobbed.

That night had seen the rug pulled from under him. If he'd found them in bed he'd probably reached for his weapon, shot the girl by mistake. She could have flung herself in front of Flake. Or been yanked there.

Her death could have put a hex on the man.

Fooling around with a woman hadn't helped Caltraine, either. He watched Tuebelo out of sight, but who could guarantee the man would stick to that course? He sure didn't want Caltraine around, and had been going to get rid of him this morning.

The girl's arrival had changed his plans but Caltraine doubted it had changed his intentions. Only so long as the girl was around could Caltraine feel safe, and not too safe at that. You could only be hung once—even for murder.

16

A repugnant thought, doubly disquieting in its shivery reminders of Broach and the badge packers hunting his whereabouts . . . the loners egged on by the size of that bounty.

There was no safety in such circumstances. Every man you bumped into was potentially an enemy, but to stay bottled up was to be a sitting duck. Tuebelo could delegate, could cock the kid and let him be the trigger. There were a half dozen ways the straw boss could handle things to get Caltraine finally out of his hair.

The only dim chance lay in flight and Caltraine knew it.

With a scowl his eyes touched the girl's, found her watching. "What is it?" she said, leaning toward him a little.

"Hobey Alred. By Tuebelo's tell he was sent to Lochiel to fetch in supplies. But Lochiel's down there—" He stabbed a hand toward the border. "A while back I turned up some fresh tracks. They were flanking the creek and headed this way." He could feel the girl's interest. "I think Alred made them."

She chewed at her lip. "You might be right. He's the only one I haven't seen around. But . . . I don't believe anyone was up on the rimrock when I came in this morning. Couldn't someone else—?"

"I've thought about that. I still think it's Alred."

"What do you suppose he's up to?"

Caltraine impatiently moved his shoulders. "The most important thing is, has the fellow left Wolftrap and—if he has—how'd he do it?"

"You think there's another way out of this basin?"

He peered into her face and could make nothing of it. For a woman she'd taken Coosie's death pretty cool. He reminded himself she was not without ambition, and could have counted him expendable when she hired him. Nothing in this deal could be taken at face value. Not even the sheriff or the things she had said of him. But he was in so deep now he had to take the gamble.

"I think we better find out. Let's pick up those tracks and see where they take us."

He got back on his horse and put him into the stream, Terry following. He was not forgetting the grim possibility that Tuebelo may have holed up someplace intending to keep an eye on them. They would not be so easily visible here and with a view of both banks they might come onto fresh sign considerably nearer than where he had originally saw it.

The trouble with suspicion was that once a man fully opened his mind to it nearly everything he looked at was colored to confirm the picture in his head.

Tuebelo fit the image she'd conjured and her impressions of the sheriff were not too unlike Caltraine's own considered opinion. A shrewd unscrupulous lawman riding roughshod over every thing and body that got in his way.

What was it the Mercantile's proprietor had said? *He's all the law we have . . . he happens also to be the topdog cattleman, owner of Chainlink.* No discrepancy there.

And Joe, Terry Ambruster had pictured as weak. Wong, on the other hand, had gratuitously told him Joe's biggest mistake was in being careless in the men he picked for friends. Which was certainly a weakness all too evident now; though, backed into Wolftrap Joe might have welcomed anyone who would help him.

Half buried back of these thoughts, Caltraine had the uncomfortable feeling all of the facts might not have been spread out yet.

He made an effort to push all this out of him. He could not afford too deep an involvement, with Broach and all the machinery of government camped on his backtrail. Crooked or otherwise, sooner or later Flake would be looking at one of those dodgers and before that happened he had better be out of here. Let Terry Ambruster find someone else if she wanted her chestnuts pulled out of the fire. No half interest in this place was worth being killed for.

If he didn't find something to put in his gun he might damn soon be dead no matter what his intentions!

They came onto fresh tracks before they'd gone half a mile.

First thing they glimpsed was damp marks drying on a shadowed piece of ledge rock. Under a bristling overhang of brush these quartered away across eroded limestone. A closer look caught the sheen of metal scratched by the slide of a horse's shoe.

Like a hound, Caltraine was up on the bank and out of the saddle. He followed this spoor to where the end of the edge went into a shale-littered run which led off to the right through a maze of cracked boulders.

Some of these blocks of stone were large as claim

shacks. They made an excellent climate for anyone seeking to trigger an ambush. Keenly aware of this, Caltraine wondered if Tuebelo was in the vicinity.

He turned to peer back across his horse at the girl, eyeing the stuffed loops of the belt round her waist, tempted to ask for a handful of cartridges. But he decided not to let her know the truth about his pistol.

Instead he said, "What makes you willing to take on a partner?"

The girl's glance went over him appraisingly. "I'm not, really. I've done it because I need a strong man. A fist to keep this outfit in hand."

"Makes sense," he said, regarding her shape with a man's appreciation. "But what do I have to show for my share?"

"Isn't my word good enough?"

"I don't know. Is it?"

She grinned at his frankness. "Looks like you'll just have to wait and see."

He said, "A man don't like to feel he's over a barrel."

"A girl doesn't care too much for that, either." She pulled her horse nearer, leaning forward to say, "How far would you trust me if our positions were reversed? I brought you into this out of desperation." She spoke with a man's directness. "But I hit on you because behind that sharp stare I felt the kind of hard strength I've seen in Ben and Tuebelo. You'll get what you want or you'll go down trying."

He told her dryly, "Let's get on with this," and returned to the saddle.

As he reined his mount forward, Caltraine thought again of those damp marks behind him. In the afternoon heat evaporation was high; it meant whoever had left them was not far ahead—Tuebelo probably.

Any damp left by Alred would have vanished long ago.

In the hours that had passed he could have been on his way back.

Caltraine impatiently sleeved whiskery cheeks. The beard he'd let grow since arriving in Wolftrap had finally got thick enough to be itchy and uncomfortable and, thus reminded of the heat, he slanched a glance overhead, startled to find the sun about to disappear behind a hurrying rack of darkly ominous clouds.

He felt like a juggler caught in a cramp with twenty-odd balls spinning over his head, and it wasn't Terry now that he was worrying about. Let her think what she wanted. Give him a chance to get out of this basin, he'd take it— straightaway if he could.

He lifted the horse into a faster gait but that which he feared was already upon them. The first big drops raised spurts of dust as they beat against the thirsty earth. The fresh trail he was following through this maze of tumbled rock would be washed out long before they could get to the end of it.

Distant thunder grumbled back of the heights and the increasing clamor of hard drumming rain swept toward them like an invisible host. Caltraine kicked heels against the sides of his laboring horse and the rain banged down with a pummeling fury.

Ahead through the downpour loomed a stretch of gray rock as wide as the horizon and thrust up into the rain for as high as he could see. A dead end, certainly, but the trail was gone and at least in the lee of those rocks they would be less exposed than they were out here. Drenched and gasping, Caltraine hurled the horse forward.

As they came under the overhang, the wind let go of them. Protected by this towering rock face they found three feet of dry ground and sat their horses hard against it, feeling like drowned rats in the plastered grip of their sopping clothes.

Caltraine felt like cursing to have come so near to what he'd been after and now had lost behind the pound of this rain. Half twisting around, he turned to see about the girl. "Don't look at me," she gasped and suddenly reached out to clutch him.

Following the startled rigidity of her stare he saw, perhaps ten yards beyond, the black maw of a hole going under the cliff.

17

"A cave!" Caltraine growled, and kneed his horse past her to pull up in front of it, excitement churning through the whole soaking length of him as he peered down into the shadowy gray depths. "By God, it's a cavern—watch your head. I'm going in."

Crouched low across the horn, he coaxed his horse into reluctant motion, descending a tortuous beaten trail that took him out of her sight into the widening dimness of an immense vaulted chamber. Off at the far side, downward slanting, was something that had the look of a passage leading between grotesque stalagmites into a kind of stygian darkness.

Terry's horse slid down under nervous urging to stop on trembling legs beside him. The girl's eyes looked bewildered, half frightened. "What is it?" she asked.

Keeping his voice down, Caltraine muttered, "I think it's how friend Alred got out of here. We can pretty soon find out."

Swinging down from the saddle, ducking round stalactities, he picked up a pitch knot from a stack against the wall. "If you're coming with me you better get down," he said, scratching a match on the leg of his Levi's.

All these exertions—all that time in the saddle—was doing him no good. At least he could be thankful his wound hadn't opened. Outside a few twinges he guessed it was lack of a square meal that was bothering him most, bringing on these spells of irritating giddiness.

When she came up beside him he handed her the torch, getting another for himself, lighting it from hers. "Look sharp now," he said, catching up his reins. "Watch your footing."

Pulling his mount along behind, he struck off into the murk through the shining ranks of crystalline deposits whose icicle-like shapes pierced the gloom all about, adding immeasurably to the macabre dance of torch-flung shadows. A creepy place. It was easy to imagine all manner of unearthly monsters with the floor slanting ever and always down like a path leading into the nethermost pit.

To Caltraine, nevertheless, this pitch was encouraging. Without it he'd have felt a great deal more dubious; if they were to find a way to the flats he'd glimpsed behind the last drop from these high piled bluffs, that way must lead downward or be useless to horsemen.

It wasn't till they'd gotten deep into this labyrinth with a good ten minutes of stiff walking behind that it occurred to Caltraine he'd been guilty of one pretty dangerous oversight.

Pushing into the mouth of this place back yonder he'd forgotten in his excitement to check on the tracks. He didn't know now if there'd been one set or two, but there was only one clear set ahead of them now.

He cursed under his breath for this mindless stupidity. How could a man with his background have been such a fool!

It was the vision of those damp marks back there on the ledge where he and Terry had come out of the stream that was pounding his skull with these klaxons of warning. Those marks simply had to have been left there by Tuebelo. Which meant, at the start, the straw boss was ahead of them.

This didn't have to mean he was ahead of them now.

Not wanting to alarm the girl unnecessarily Caltraine pushed on, but the nag of his thoughts presently forced him to stop and get down on one knee in the dust of the trail for a closer look. There was no doubt about it. Only one set of tracks overlay all the rest. These pointed in the direction Caltraine was going and, near as he could determine, they were several hours old.

So where in the bloody hell was Tuebelo?

If he'd seen them come in he'd be back of them someplace. Caltraine twisted his head for a look, seeing the girl's white face peering down at him. "What is it?" she whispered, and the cavern whispered round her.

Caltraine shook his head. "Just checking," he answered, and got back on his feet with increased apprehensions. He caught up his reins and set off again, angrily watchful, knowing he'd put them both in a bind—a trap that if sprung could leave their bones in its jaws.

It wasn't a happy thought, but if Tuebelo was back of them—this appeared too certain to be open to question—Alred's return, unless they got out of here before he came in, was apt to find them wedged like kippered herring in a grocer's box.

His only visible chance—and it looked powerfully thin—depended on getting out of this before Alred arrived.

Easier said than done, he imagined. There might be other ways out of this labyrinth; they'd passed several dark corridors wandering off to left and right, but where these led he'd no means of knowing. Like as not most of them wound up against blank walls.

He was rather sorely tempted to try one, regardless. Any port in a storm, sailors said. But he wasn't a sailor and this wasn't the sea. He was a badly rattled gambler reduced to one white chip.

They could take one of these blind alleys and, far enough back to be out of light's reach, crouch there in black like the bottom of a mine and hope like hell whoever passed would not discover them. This was what any wise mouse would do but it was not a comparison to please a man's fancy and Tuebelo, if he was bent on a showdown, would have an eye cocked for any sign that turned off.

If they were forced into one of these side corridors Caltraine aimed for it to be one a great deal nearer to the outside than this. Were he given any choice he would sooner test his luck against Hobey Alred in or out than be cornered by Tuebelo.

In the midst of these anxieties he could still find scope to wool over several irrelevant thoughts. Like the choices he'd had on the night of that card game before quitting Prescott—even after he'd cut loose. There were hundreds of miles of land to get lost in but always Pine Knob at the back of his thinking, pulling him on like a blind man's dog.

Had he stopped someplace else he never would have gotten mixed up with this filly. If he'd first come onto her at Ambruster's stage depot was it likely she'd have talked him into coming out here?

Seen in the clarity of hindsight everything appeared to have conspired to put him into this. Joe's brutal slaying, the girl spun off her feet by that stage horse, the bullypuss sheriff and his highhanded ultimatum . . . the girl waylaying him just as he was figuring to pull out with Wong's grubstake. His reception at Wolftrap. Tuebelo.

He shook off these thoughts. He was here—you couldn't get around that. What he had to do now was find a way to get out. No need to blame Terry, he told himself testily. From the time he had got himself into long pants most of the hectic things that had happened had stemmed from pretty faces—you would think he'd have learned from that trouble with Broach!

He pushed on now with a greater impatience, passing two more turnoffs. All he had to do now was find the end of this passage, get out on the flats and start heating his axles.

Probably it wasn't going to be quite that easy. The girl almost certainly would set up a squawk. Time enough to wrangle about that when they got there.

They must have come the biggest part of a mile. Mostly the route had seemed reasonably straight, with no sharp twists of which he'd been aware. In prehistoric times, he reckoned, this might have been the channel of some underground river.

A bat came swooping past his torch and in these magnified acoustics he heard the girl's startled gasp. He took a faster gait, impatient to be out of this, convinced what he sought could not be far away. The blackness seemed thicker, somehow different up ahead, and as they neared he found himself peering at what was obviously solid rock.

The shock of this rooted him till his stare picked up the churn of tracks and Terry, again beside him, said, "Off there—" and turned him with a tug at his shoulder.

The trail at this point had gone off at right angles and there, ahead perhaps two hundred yards, he saw a grayness like false dawn illuminating another twist in the passage.

He caught her eye and bent to snuff his torch. But with not enough dirt underfoot for the purpose, he stamped at its flame and flung it behind him, the girl reluctantly following suit. "Come on," he said, and struck off again.

She caught up with him, hauling her nervous gelding, and was starting to speak when he brusquely shushed her.

In the pull of the brightening light up ahead they passed another side passage opening off to the left, but Caltraine gave it scant notice in his hurry.

He could feel the pry of her stare digging into him but wouldn't let himself turn lest she stop him to talk up some fool woman notion. There would be time aplenty to listen to her jawing when she saw him making ready to take off. He reckoned she would have some things to say about that.

But first things first, and the first thing here was to get out from the squeezed-in walls of this cavern while he still had steam enough left to do it.

It had sure as hell narrowed down considerably. The roof was still out of sight high above but the sides of this passage had bent near enough together that there was barely room to squeeze horses by. There were droppings on the floor though, proof sufficient that someone had rode through.

He came up toward the place of strongest light and found, as he'd suspected, another blind corner. Here the passage made a left bend where some terrible force in ages past had thrust its way through rotten rock to burst at last onto open flats.

Pulled up to stare, he had just let go of his choked-back breath when they caught the sound of approaching hooves.

18

In the echoing chamber it was not at once evident whether the sound came from in front or behind. But Caltraine had the wit to stay where he was, crouched in the elbow of this shadowy passage, ready on cue to duck either way.

Eyes bleak in the frozen mask of his face, he watched for a sign, every faculty honed to razor edge.

He did not attempt to divide his attention. His glance stayed glued to the brush-screened opening eighty feet ahead. He was sure the sound was coming from outside. No man with all his marbles was going to be approaching those abandoned, still-flickering torches on the back of any horse.

He knew without looking that the girl was beside him. She'd be frightened, hardly knowing up from down and this, for the moment was just the way he wanted it. The crux of his plan depended on it.

When the first slanch of shadow impinged on the foliage-blocked opening, Caltraine whirled in his tracks, right arm stabbing out to spin the girl even as his left snaked the pistol from her holster. "Back!" he gruffed. "Quick—*round the bend!*" He gave her a shove, snatching both sets of reins to haul the nervous horses along.

Even if he'd thought to look, Caltraine was fairly sure Alred hadn't seen them; he could think of no reason for the man to be suspicious. Thrusting her horse's reins at the girl, Caltraine whispered, "We better muzzle these broncs and get out of sight. Try that tunnel on the right, that one just ahead of you."

He was a little surprised that she obeyed so meekly. He'd expected an argument. Pushing her ahead of him, both of them feeling their way with held breaths, Caltraine got his party clear of the main passage.

Not satisfied with this, he kept them moving for as long as he dared, wanting to get them round a bend out of sight. But they still hadn't found anything that would hide them aside from the perpetual night of this place when, pulled up in a tenseness of nervous listening, they heard the loudening approach of a walking horse.

In this echoing vault it was impossible to tell if he were in the main passage. Too keyed up just to wait for fate to hit him, Caltraine pushed Terry's shoulder, urging her on, counting on Alred's own noise to cover them.

But the girl wouldn't move. Her hand instead, taking hold of his, pushed it past and ahead of her, thrusting it roughly against solid rock.

Pain told him better than spoken words they had run out of running room; they had used up this tunnel. He was turning around when Alred's horse nickered.

Caltraine grabbed his mount's nostrils.

For a long stretch of moments there were no other sounds.

It wasn't hard to imagine Alred back there gone stiff as a doorpost, head full of questions and a gun in his fist.

Horses generally didn't nicker just to hear their heads rattle.

Alred struck him as a man who'd been around enough to know.

Why hadn't he made a light? Had something before this roused his suspicions?

When Caltraine's horse tried to shake its head he eased his grip a little, ready to clamp again if the animal showed any sign of giving voice.

The furtive quiet ran on, steeped in menace till it seemed this very stillness must in the end betray them through its cruel tax on nerves.

And where all this while was Tuebelo? What was he doing back there in the dark beyond the dim flare of that pair of dropped torches? With the sound of that horse still ringing through his head he'd be doubly reluctant to be caught in their light. It would smell too much like a trap—it was bound to.

Caltraine realized then if any light still showed from those discarded pitch knots Alred must certainly have glimpsed its reflection. That he had not was apparent in the racket his mount had raised.

Hard on the heels of this conclusion it crossed Caltraine's mind that the both of them, likely, were as mixed up as he was. He at least, if this deal touched off gunplay, didn't have to be anxious lest he cut down a friend.

The sudden rasp of a match reversed the whole concept. This burst of light—small though it was and probably cupped—ripping across what had been black as jet developed the facts like a flash of forked lightning.

There was no one in sight, not even the match or the bastardly hand that had crazily struck it. Nothing to look at but the creep of a shadow across the damp shine of the tunnel's left wall where it joined the main passage less than forty feet away.

Then the light was gone and the black was back, twice as deep and crammed with a menace immeasurably greater as Caltraine, haunted by the creep of that shadow, reached out for the girl and touched nothing at all.

In the bitterness of resentment he almost cursed aloud. Then his hand, encountering the flinching rump of her horse, passed gingerly down a trembling hind leg over fetlock and hoof to furiously close on the still-warm leather of discarded boots. Was there, by God, no end to her perfidy?

He could guess what she'd done.

On the stealth of bare feet she'd slipped off to trade sides again to make whatever deal looked best to guarantee her investment.

The weight of her gun in his sweating right fist suggested he might get in a few licks before he was left for the coyotes, but it sure burned him up to be thrown over this way. Did she think him a fool to be caught with his pants down?

He hadn't escaped Broach to be pinned in a corner!

Taking a hitch in his temper he considered the angles and found he still had some cards up his sleeve. He could stampede these horses, send them helter-skelter out into that passage and maybe force enough slack to let him get out of here.

He was gathering the reins to loop them over the horns when he heard the girl call in a sob of desperation, "Alred! *Is that you?*"

In the inky black he could hear her flopping around like a cat in a sack trying to claw her way out. Curiosity held him through a mounting excitement. What kind of game was she playing at now?

"Alred—" She gasped in a muffled-up frenzy. "It's Terry *Ambruster*, Alred. . . . You're not afraid of me, are you?"

The silence grew thick with unspoken suspicions. Caltraine stood fiercely gripped to his pistol. "What's up?" Alred's voice said. There was no scuff of movement.

"That crazy damn Walters! The one I sent out here—"

"What about him?"

"I was showing him around; he'd some stupid idea Flake might get at our water. We were following the creek when he came onto your tracks and discovered this passage. He insisted we explore it. After we got in here he tied me up and took off."

The silence closed in again. Scarcely breathing, Caltraine waited. The girl made more struggling thumps. When she quit Alred said flatly, "Where are you?"

"In some kind of tunnel. Just off the trail. Make a light and you'll see me."

19

Alred said, "Might be I'd see somethin' I wouldn't cotton to." Whatever his faults the man was no dimwit. This much was apparent when, voice thinning, he growled, "No one come past me."

"You don't see him here now, do you?"

"I ain't fixin' to, either."

"Are you intending to leave me tied here all night?"

It got no change out of Alred. It was shaping up, Caltraine thought, to be a Mexican standoff. Unless the fellow stepped over to where he could be got at they were no further along than before she'd gone out there.

Terry, not attempting to scale down her feelings, cried: "Go find Tuebelo—*he*'ll get me out of this. And when he does, Hobey Alred, you'll—"

"Wouldn't count on that," Alred said. "What did this Walters do with your horses?"

"How would *I* know?" she snapped back at him, exasperated. "Way it sounded I'd say he took them with him when he went tearing off up this tunnel."

The silence picked up again. Caltraine could imagine Alred standing there turning this over. Things were beginning to fuzz round the edges and Caltraine wondered if he was about to be light-headed again ˉwhen Alred finally spoke. "Up that tunnel, eh?"

"If you had a little gumption you could quick enough find out. I don't suppose he bothered to rub out his tracks."

"With you on the job I don't guess he'd need to."

"What's that supposed to mean?"　ˋ

"For your information, missy, I could reach the end of that tunnel with a throw rope."

Caltraine, in his weakness, dared wait no longer. He didn't know where Tuebelo was but it was plenty apparent Alred had no intention of swapping his advantage for a clout on the head.

Letting go of the horses—he couldn't stampede them with the girl in their path—he began to edge forward. Terry had said she was just inside the tunnel. If he could reach the intersection without discovery it was possible he could put the girl's gun to use and, given luck enough, get them out of this jackpot.

He felt his way along the wall under cover of her renewed squirming. His mind rebelled at the caution forced upon him, at the infinite care his slowed responses made advisable. He wanted to hurl himself out there and have this over with, but he was shrewd enough to know that getting himself killed wasn't what he was looking for.

He was still ten feet from the passage hiding Alred when the man remarked, "I'm goin' to stay right here till you come out of there, Walters."

"Then you'll be there a mighty while," Terry said.

"I can wait as long as he can."

Pressure folded in the corners of Caltraine's lips. The truth of that was galling. He was finding it harder to keep his wits about him. He didn't have forever.

Decision was taken out of his hands when one of the hitched horses in back of him pawed ground, nickering. Alred's mount was quick to reply.

Caltraine said, "Will money get you off my back?"

Judgment vindicated, Alred chuckled. "Last I heard, you didn't have any money, sport."

"The picture's changed since you last saw him," Terry answered. "He's got back that eighty thousand."

Alred sounded a mocking whistle. "You catch Tuebelo with his eyes shut?"

Caltraine scratched at the itch of his whiskers. "I've got the money. Belt and all."

"Mister, I'm from Missouri. You want a deal, throw it out."

The belt was stuffed with bills but there was hard money too. They all heard the clink when it landed in the passage.

Alred said, "Now the guns."

Swearing wasn't going to change anything. Caltraine, scowling, chucked out his empty pistol.

Alred said, "What about the rifle?"

"Didn't bring one."

"Reckon she forgot to fetch hers too. Where's her hogleg?"

Terry said sarcastically, "How do you think I can pitch a gun when I can't even get on my feet tied up this way?"

"If he tied you up he sure wasn't fool enough to leave you with anything handy as a pistol. Throw it out here, sport."

"That wasn't part of the deal."

"I'm dealin' now. I been around somethin' more than a fortnight or two. You don't think I'd reach for that belt with you armed, do you?"

"You going to ride off and leave it laying there?"

Alred chuckled. "Guess that's one of them rhetorical questions. How you fixin' to get it back without steppin' out where I can get at you?"

"Was hoping for that much dinero you'd be willing to ride off and forget you ever saw me."

"Nothin' like hope. So do yourself a favor and let's quit horsin' round. I'm not movin' one foot till you pitch that gun out here."

"Then we might's well sit down," Caltraine said, hanging onto his patience.

"You don't sound so good, sport. How's that hurt standin' up to this exercise? Want to sink your choppers in a thick juicy steak?"

That fellow wasn't talking just to hear if he still had a voice. Kind of seemed someway like the sound of it was nearer.

Caltraine, keeping his mouth shut, edged gingerly forward. If surprises were in the offing he didn't mean for them all to turn up on one side.

"You outsmarted yourself when you put that silly bitch out there for decoy," Alred said craftily. "She'll be right in your way if you try bustin' out of this on one of them horses. But I don't care if you don't. Come any time you've a mind to."

Covered by this babble Caltraine had felt his way to the junction. He was reasonably sure Alred had done the same, which, if correct, put the pair of them now within arm's reach of each other, with nothing but the wall's rock corner between where they crouched and the inevitable shootout.

The day, Caltraine reckoned, must be pretty well shot. Near as Terry must be to him now he was not able to make out her shape in this murk, and the dark of this place seemed not a whit lighter when he peered toward where the passage, presumably, debouched on the flats he had looked at from the top of the bluffs. This would be counted in his favor if he grabbed a horse and tried to get out of here.

An involuntary shiver jerked at his sinews, but it was the coldness of tension rather than fear. Unless Tuebelo put in to take chips in this set-to Caltraine reckoned his chances to be about as good as Alred's. Providing, of course, his hard punished body didn't cross him up or conk out just when the going got roughest.

He couldn't bank on the speed of his reflexes, so it was plain he'd have to assume the initiative. He could not afford, certainly, to stand around waiting for Alred to come after him.

Only one course of action offered the prospect of success. He would have to round this corner shooting and trust that one of his slugs would find its mark. A gamble? Sure, but all of life was a gamble and if he could encompass the advantage of surprise he could drop the man before Alred got in his licks. It was the only thing he had left to count on.

But the plan had one drawback and this was what bothered him: Tuebelo's whereabouts. He had no way of knowing where the straw boss was, and it would do him no good to cut down Alred only to be dropped in turn by the gun of Tuebelo.

And it could easily happen—it was in the cards.

He could minimize this if he got down on his belly, but he knew he just wasn't up to any lengthy maneuvering.

He drew a nervous breath and carefully gathered himself. He was up on his toes, taut and ready for the try, when saddle leather creaked somewhere back there in the black. Before he was able to grasp its significance a horse lunged past him wildly.

20

Though it scared the living hell out of him, Caltraine didn't wait but straightaway flung himself round the rock face into a passage now murkily lit by the flame-tongued flare of Alred's frantically thundering shots.

The man was crouched hard against the near wall, jerking convulsively, one arm thrown up, jaws wide with his yell, as Caltraine's slugs punched into him. With the third, he bent, then his knees let go. Caltraine was already whirling, to stumble after the girl, when the man's lifeless body fell inertly by his hat.

With the last clattery echoes of those powder bursts subsiding, Caltraine quit his futile groping to listen. All he could hear was the thud of his heart. Unless she'd got out, her horse wasn't moving.

Was she down? Had one of those wild shots gone ripping into her?

His legs felt unwieldy as a pair of damned stilts and a thousand confusions seized hold of him. In the smothering folds of this tomblike dark he was suddenly aware, in the midst of his uncertainties, of having just about lost all sense of direction.

Too damned weak to take another step, he was sorely tempted to let go all holds and abandon himself to the blessed relief of encroaching oblivion.

It was the nearest he'd come to the end of his rope. In this terrible inertia of near exhaustion not even the sardonic face of Tuebelo sliding in and out of his ken like a wraith was able to provoke but a mumbled oath. Only one thing kept him on his feet, an inescapable conviction that the girl had put her life on the line to afford him the chance of coming out on top of that set-to with Alred.

He slammed into a wall and the shock of it brought things into grim focus. If nothing else those shots must have alerted the straw boss. If he was ever to get out of this goddamn labyrinth it would sure have to be before Tuebelo got here.

He foggily remembered that before this near blackout he had been someplace nearer the exit than the juncture of the tunnel. Thing to do, then, was follow the wall. If it took him north he was bound to come to where it debouched on the flats.

All set to go, he remembered the horse he'd left back there. He made a considerable effort to pull himself together.

He needed that horse more than a gun right now. He'd have to go back for it.

Shaken by the thought, he finally stumbled into motion.

It couldn't have been more than a handful of yards, but it seemed to Caltraine he must be groping through eternity before his outstretched hand lost contact with the wall. His sense of balance failed to support him and he wound up sprawled on the passage floor.

He may have passed out. The reproachful whinny of a horse pulled his cheek from the dust and he staggered to his feet, glance wildly raking the impenetrable dark. Memory crept back in bits and pieces, and one of those pieces was the picture of his bankroll laying around in this blackness someplace. He felt around with his feet and heard the clink as his foot nudged it.

He bent over and came up with it dangling. The other fist, when he tried to put the thing round him, seemed unconscionably heavy and useless till he remembered it was still holding Terry's shooter.

It took another endless while to presently stash this in his waistband and get the stuffed belt buckled over it. The horse stomped impatiently and blew through its nostrils. "Yeah . . . I'm comin'," Caltraine muttered.

He found the reins, took a pull on the horn and after three tries half fell across the saddle. He was too spent to think of guiding the horse; it was pure bull luck he didn't go banging his head into something. By the time his precarious position was evident, they were moving through brush. It was the scrape of thorny branches that painfully roused him to the feel of night wind blowing across his damp skin.

They were out in the open before his feet found the stirrups and he could prod himself upright for a bleary look around.

The horse under him had stopped, scarcely three feet short of another standing crossways, its rider somewhat familiar.

Caltraine had to look twice to pull her name from the clutter of pounding thoughts and find in the whirling sequence of recollected events a niche she would properly fit. Then the mists cleared a bit and he found himself returning her stare, trying to see past the words that were tumbling about him. When he sorted them out and strung them together they still didn't make very much of an impression.

"Are you all right?" she asked, voice concerned. "I was just about to go back and start hunting you."

He grunted, "Yeah," and wished her face would stand

still long enough to get a fix on it. "You're the Ambruster girl," he growled, vaguely surprised, and couldn't think why this should bother him.

There was something about the way she kept watching him which clawed at the edge of his unstable faculties, but his damn fuzzy thoughts couldn't pin the thing down. She said, "We'd better get back," and, when he kept peering stupidly, "You're not about to let him get away with this, are you?"

He felt the shove of her horse against the side of his leg. It got through to him presently the girl had been shaking him. "Walters!" she cried, and he threw off her hand. Then her face got real close. "Can you hear me?"

"Course I can hear."

"Then what are you staring for? There was supposed to be only one way into Wolftrap. Now we know that's not so, that Tuebelo was aware of it—doesn't that suggest anything to you, Walters?"

Caltraine shrugged. But his mind was clearer. "Expect he reckons to take the place over."

"It suggests to me Joe was playing into more than hard luck when he walked into that bind and got himself killed. It looks to me like he was damn well *framed!*"

"I'll ride with that," Caltraine said.

"Then he's got to be dealt with." She caught hold of his arm in the grip of her emotions, but Caltraine said, "You're not getting me back into that place again!"

She dropped the arm, shocked. The moon came out from a tumble of clouds and showed her face clearly, showed the primitive frantic compulsions twisting her but did not change his intentions one whit.

"But half the place is yours—"

He shook his head. "I've got no use for it."

He could see by the way her eyes squeezed down she wasn't going to take that remark at face value. She said,

"You can't run out on me now. I meant what I said: You can write your own ticket."

He looked at her face, the lush curves of her figure. It was plain what she was offering but, "The answer's no," he said to her flatly. "If you want the place, make your deals with Tuebelo. He's bossing that outfit; don't ever think different."

"But it's *mine!*" she cried, furious.

He felt stirrings of pity. How hard it was if you had never had much to see the little you had counted on moved out of reach. But it wasn't his fight. He didn't want any part of it, and picked up his reins.

"Wait—" she called sharply. "Where are you off to?"

He looked at her squarely. "I doubt that he'll give a damn, just so I go."

"It's not him who'll want to stop you, and I wouldn't tell him anyway."

He rubbed a hand across his jaw, seeing the bleakness back of that stare, remembering the crazy risk she had taken to distract Hobey Alred in his behalf. "I'd be no good to you, Terry."

She said in a swift, aggressive way: "Have you forgotten Ben Flake? He'll never let you ride out."

21

He thought about that, slowly shaking his head. "I'll be out of his jurisdiction by morning."

"Not in the shape you're in, you won't. Not by yourself. I doubt you ever set eyes on Arivaca. Ruby, maybe but not Arivaca—it's the longest part of fifty miles. Use your head!"

His mulish look appeared to anger her suddenly. She said, kneeing her mount alongside, "All right, darn you. I'll go that far—"

"Why?"

Below the odd zircon-like color of baffling eyes her dark lips bent in a secretive smile. He said, "Don't you reckon that would be kind of foolish?"

"Let's just say I owe you that much."

"You don't owe me a thing."

"A lot could happen in fifty miles. That's a pretty dry stretch across there, Walters. You'll not see many people and those you might will be the kind to shoot first and talk later."

His mouth showed impatience. "You'd be no help."

The moon, slipping in and out of wind-tossed clouds, set up glints of mahogany in the tumbled look of her chestnut hair. Her hands, now folded over the horn, stirred restively. Eyeing her, he felt the pull of something he did not care to recognize and threw at her irritably: "I don't want you with me!"

"You want to wind up out there someplace *dead*? At least I know where the waterholes are."

"You're not changing my mind." He pulled his mount's head around, kicked the horse into a lope and pointed its nose toward the dark line of hills shimmering wraithlike just over the horizon.

"You'll wind up in Tubac," she called, reining after him, "if you stay on that course. Arivaca's farther into the west."

He pulled his horse over, too beat to argue. He could not afford to be seen in Tubac. Not too long ago that cotton-wood shaded town on the river had been the Territory's capital and more than just a few of its residents kept shrewd hands on the pulse of politics in the forlorn hope that one of these days they'd have the government back.

His head was too filled with a hodgepodge of thoughts to leave any room for the shaping of plans, even had such been practical at this stage. He didn't reckon Tuebelo would feel called upon to take after him, but Flake might prove a different kettle of fish.

If, as contended, Flake was using his office to feather his nest it seemed likely enough he wouldn't be wanting the fact spread around. He might even imagine this Vic Walters hombre to be some kind of snooper sent in to look things over.

But Terry had her own ax to grind. She wanted his help to take over and hang onto that outfit of Joe's; for all he knew she might even have a right to it. But only a plumb idiot in Caltraine's fix would risk being stuck in a place like Wolftrap with a badge like Flake all set to clamp down.

He could hear her spurring after him. You had to give her E for effort. Right or wrong she knew what she wanted and had the guts to go after it. He called over his shoulder, "You're just wasting your time."

He might as well not have spoken. She kept right on coming. When she pulled up alongside he let his gelding drop back into a lope. Most of the rain, by the look of this ground, appeared to have fallen south of the bluffs; out here on these flats it hadn't even laid the dust.

Her reminder of his condition did nothing to improve his outlook. He felt like he'd been pulled through a knot hole, but Broach was the spur that had its hooks in him now. He simply could not afford to be trapped at Wolftrap.

He slanced another look at her. "I suppose you can go anywhere you've a mind to, but sticking with me won't buy you a thing."

She kept her face straight front.

Jugheaded as a mule, Caltraine told himself bitterly. Then he said, "You've pinned your hopes to the wrong man, Terry. It ain't in the cards for me to go back. I'm on the run—"

"That's why I reckoned we'd be good for each other. You could hole up at Wolftrap. . . ."

He snarled, "That's just what I *can't* do. You got a fight coming on and a sheriff mixed up in it. Flake and Tuebelo! Pair like that could bust this wide open. Half the Territory's camped on my shirttail—I'm hunting a hole, not a goddamn showcase!"

She said, "That sounds like murder."

"That's what they've called it."

"Can't see that you've much to lose in that case." She said, cool as a well chain, "You can only swing once."

"That's a comforting thought."

She had her own thoughts. "We could win this fight—"

"Not me," Caltraine snapped, at the end of his patience. "I've never got into a hero's shirt and, believe me, I ain't about to. I'm getting out of this country. Fast as this goddamn bronc'll take me."

It was an excellent decision straight from the shoulder but, like a lot of fine notions, a bit premature. Almost before the words were out, the girl, swinging toward him, clutched at his arm.

But he was already staring where her own eyes were focused at the dark line of horsemen spurring out of a wash half a mile ahead, spreading rapidly in front of them to block off their advance.

He counted ten of them and blackly cursed when, toting up the chances, he realized they hadn't even one in five of getting past that expanding line. With a half mile lead they could close every gap.

Caltraine pulled up, the girl beside him. "Looks like Flake's horse there in the lead—that claybank. And that black right behind looks like Virgil Bond's—he's the Pine Knob blacksmith. He wouldn't be with them if this was Flake's Chainlink outfit."

"What would Flake be doing out here with a posse?"

"Don't ask me to read his mind. You fixing to make a run for it?"

"We'll have to turn back," Caltraine said.

He whirled his mount, the girl following suit, and headed for the blue stretch of bluffs he'd so thankfully quit hardly more than one short hour before. With the moon full upon them, he scanned them intently but failed to find anything which looked like a break. Rising sheer from the flats, the bluffs stretched right and left in immeasurable miles. He peered over his shoulder and cursed again.

The bunch spurring back of them were swinging their quirts. There could no longer be any doubt of their intentions. Whatever had fetched them, their plain purpose now was centered in overtaking Terry and Caltraine.

"Any way around those cliffs?" he called sharply.

The girl shook her head. "We wouldn't have time. We've got fresher horses, but if we turn they'll shortcut and catch us." She smiled thinly. "Our only chance now is to get back to Wolftrap."

22

Caltraine's look was black, but there was no sense in fighting it. If he wanted to stay out of the hands—and he did—the only thing left was to heat up their axles.

He drove the horse harder.

The obvious answer to the posse's presence had to lie in that trip Hobey Alred had taken. Either Tuebelo had sprung some kind of a deal or Alred himself had sold out the lot of them. If the sheriff had known of this hidden way in, his squabble with Wolftrap would have been wound up long ago.

The question now was how to keep them *out*.

Once in the cavern with Alred's rifle he could probably stand them off, but how long he could do this was certainly debatable. In the shape he was in, it was stretching his luck pretty thin to believe he could hold this passage till the girl reached Tuebelo and got back with help. *And how much help could he figure to count on?*

Precious damn little when you came right down to it.

Tuebelo, certainly, if he hadn't engineered this. Possibly one other, the Ruddabaugh kid or timid Gurd Bedderman if one or the other of them happened to be available. He wouldn't get both because somebody had to be up in the rimrocks holding the front door shut. And even if Tuebelo had had nothing to do with the approach of this bunch the girl might not be able to find him.

It didn't look good any way you cut it.

The most obvious choice for rotten apple was Tuebelo. Nobody else had the reasons that he had, the all-consuming hatred or the readiness for risk. No one else in Joe's crew had been posted for murder.

To that extent, anyway, Caltraine and the straw boss were in the same fix. Dead or alive, the law wanted both of them. But even in this there was no feel of kinship.

Caltraine wasn't burning to get back at anyone. No need for revenge was tearing him apart, no festering hate red-fogging his judgments. His way of life—all his holdings—hadn't been swept away by any badge-wearing friend for the murder of a girl he'd had his heart set on marrying.

No man driven by those kind of thoughts would ever be wholly rational or held by the tenets which served other men. In a pinch such a man would be no more predictable than that crazy, unstable kid. Put those two aside and who was there left that he could send the girl after? No one but Bedderman, a weak chinned jasper who looked scared of his shadow.

Caltraine had sure wedged himself between a rock and a hard place!

Distances by moonlight were inclined to be deceptive but the look of those cliffs—despite the pace they were setting —did not seem appreciably nearer. The only encouragement apparent was that, so far anyway as pursuit was concerned, they appeared to be holding their own in this race. He almost dared think they might have gained a few rods.

But this wasn't much help against the facts he'd be faced with when it came to keeping this bunch out of Wolftrap.

One man in the mouth of that tunnel might be able to hold off an army, providing his grub and his cartridges held out. Only he didn't think he was that man.

A job of that kind called for unceasing vigilance, a cool he didn't have in his present condition—nor was that *all* he didn't have. Half starved already, he had no prospect of food. The rifle shells he'd got from Wong and distributed among his pockets had been taken with the belts before Joe's crew had brought him round. He'd gotten back his bankroll but there were just two cartridges left in Terry's pistol between them and ignominious surrender.

He pushed his horse still harder with these bleak facts confronting him, knowing he had to pile up enough lead to get into that tunnel, find Alred's rifle and get back to the brush-screened mouth of that cavern before Flake's posse came slam-banging in.

He put all his will to it.

In this kind of country a man didn't sacrifice a horse without he had to. But when it came to a choice between a mount and his own life no one but a fool was going to hesitate a minute.

The girl's mount was beginning to show signs of flagging but he could see the wind-tossed line of that brush now and, knowing he hadn't any time for sentiment, called on the sorrel for all the drive he could get.

Two hundred yards . . . a hundred . . . fifty. Above the rush and pound of hooves thrown back by the cliffs was a cork-stopper popping that drove him down against the lathered neck.

Then they were tearing through the brush's thorny branches, hunting the black maw of that cavern.

The horse flung up his head and reared back, snorting, not at all inclined toward any further sampling of the terrors of that passage. Caltraine, in no mood for foolishness, hammered him back of the ears with the heel of his fist, at the same time raking him hard with the steel. The sorrel, still snorting, plunged into the black as Terry came up on her floundering mount.

He pushed on toward the bend through thickening shadows, all his hopes grimly pinned to finding on Alred enough rifle fodder to give the girl, anyway, some kind of start. With her horse blowing hard, they came into the first elbow; the sorrel, edgy, still reluctantly advancing, bunched up as though, given half a chance, he would bolt at any moment.

With the bend put behind, they came into the solid black where he had shot it out with Alred and there Caltraine swung down. "Get off," he said, and heard her saddle creak. He passed her his reins. "I'm going to try to keep that bunch out of here. You take my horse and try to find us some help."

"You can't hold them off with a pistol—"

"I'll have Alred's rifle," he growled impatiently, boosting her into the saddle. "We've no time to argue. Send the kid if you can find him—now get out of here." He brought a hand smartly against the sorrel's rump.

He stepped back, head cocked, to listen as the horse took off with Terry. The other horse, still breathing hard, stood in its tracks, head hanging, too spent even to whinny. And this pulled Caltraine's head around, sending his stare stabbing into the dark.

There was nothing to hear beyond the sorrel's departure. Why wasn't Alred's horse sounding off? Caltraine whipped a match across the leg of his Levi's and softly cursed as the flame raveled out.

Alred's horse was gone. And Alred with him. And, worst of all, the man's rifle and cartridges.

In the bludgeoning dismay it didn't matter how or where. There were just two shots in the wheel of Terry's pistol and ten men outside spurred by Flake's orders to get into Wolftrap.

He palmed the girl's six-shooter, rounding the bend, and ran toward the moonlit shape of the cavern mouth. The racket of approaching horsemen was loud as it banged back and forth against the rock of these walls. He had no hope at all they wouldn't find the entrance; they'd been carefully coached or they'd not have been out there.

Two shots!

Even if he brought down a man with each there'd still be eight left to pound his hide into doll rags. Pressured by desperation, he toted up his chances and feverishly sought some way out of this corner. Giving up wasn't going to do him any good. Flake, by this time, would have one of those dodgers. Even if he hadn't there were other scores to settle. Who could look for lenience in a sheriff of Flake's caliber?

That sonofabitch was going to ride right over him! Unless—

Caltraine blinked as a wild thought hit him. If he could manage to take Flake out of this . . .

23

Stopped by the thought, he stood hung over the dangling weight of Terry's near-emptied pistol, listening to horse sounds and breaking brush. Overriding all was the battering flail of Flake's roughshod orders bullying the men on, patiently pushing them into a search for the hole he seemed certain had swallowed their quarry.

"It's in there someplace! Here's where we lost sight of them. Get off those damn broncs and start beating that brush!"

"What's the matter with burnin' it?" somebody called.

"I don't care how you do it—just find me that hole!"

An ominous crackle of spreading flames broke across Caltraine's hearing. A flickering glow began to pick out the walls and the smell of burning wood became suddenly stronger as a fresh wind sucked a string of smoke past Caltraine's cheeks.

He backed away from it, grimacing, fist fiercely tightening round the grip of his pistol.

In no time at all the only thing he could hear was the roar coming off that burning brush. Now it was the heat that drove him back, but only momentarily because, in spite of the smoke, he could see well enough that once the flames had done their work Flake would have that whole push bundling in here.

The only chance of effecting any part of a surprise would be right at the start, before their eyes grew adjusted to the difference in light.

Getting down on all fours put him out of the smoke and the worst of the heat. But knowing he could not afford to take root there, he sidled over till he touched the right-hand wall, then worked his way gingerly along this toward the blazing inferno of the flame-choked outlet.

Twenty feet from the brightness, eyes squinted nearly shut and the skin of his face feeling like it was being peeled off him in strips, he backed into a niche that shielded him somewhat. He wondered how much chance he'd have when the rush came, to pick off the sheriff.

He didn't put much stock in the possibilities; a fellow like Flake wasn't going to lead no rush if he could bludgeon others into it. And once they got in here, Caltraine grimly reckoned, he wouldn't be given much choice about where he put those bullets. He'd better fire straightaway or he wouldn't get to at all.

It was getting darker in here with the shadows creeping back, congealing, as the fire burned down. Pretty soon now Flake would be sending them in, driving them before him—he was that kind of pelican. He just about had to be to pull the kind of thing the girl had said he had on Tuebelo.

The shadows now were all about. Caltraine braced himself as best he could, knowing he hadn't much longer to wait, hoping the girl had got out of the passage and was flogging her horse in a run for the ranch. Not that any help she might find was like to get back in time for the showdown—it wasn't in the cards if he was reading them right.

The chances of Alred having brought Flake down on them looked too negligible to seriously consider. He *might* have done it, but in Caltraine's view it had to be Tuebelo. What the man stood to gain wasn't presently apparent. Any trade he could have offered simply wouldn't stand up once the sheriff got into this basin with a posse, and Tuebelo must know this.

Perhaps all he wanted was to get Flake into his gunsights, which was all Caltraine wanted right now, too.

He could hear the sheriff's voice snarling, the creaking of leather as the posse, plainly without much enthusiasm, climbed into saddles. "I'll be right behind you," Flake told them pointedly.

The sounds of walking horses drew nearer. Caltraine's length settled into a crouch. The palms of his hands felt slippery with sweat.

The passage entrance darkened with the approaching shapes of bent-forward horsemen. No one seemed anxious to find himself in the lead. They milled there uncertainly, backing and fiddling while the tension piled up and the need to do something nearly set Caltraine crazy. The sound of a gun being cocked broke the impasse and two horsebackers moved into sight, rifles held ready as their eyes raked the gloom.

Sure they would spot him, it took all the will Caltraine could lay hold of to keep his grip off that trigger as the pair moved deeper into the passage, propelled by the surge of horsemen behind.

Two more appeared as Caltraine's pistol—monstrous as cannon fire in these close confines—released both bullets.

Out of that bedlam of horse sounds and shouting came the battering impact of roaring Winchesters. Both lead riders were swept from their hulls as the terrified animals bolted from under them. A horse went down whickering pitifully as Caltraine plunged from his niche to fling himself forward, both hands scrabbling, straightening up with a rifle which he fired point-blank into that swirling confusion of cursing men and frantic animals.

A man wildly yelling, with arms outflung, was cata- pulted off the back of his mount and lost in the melee of twisting shapes that were jammed in the exit, caught in blind panic by the slamming reports.

When the rifle was empty Caltraine crouched, almost unbelieving, as with still churning guts he peered across dark lumps at the trafficless alley between himself and that motionless patch of moonlit desert.

It outraged intelligence to believe such a holocaust could actually be over with himself still upright and apparently unscathed.

The posse, of course, had panicked, convinced like enough they'd walked into an ambush, and Flake might be figuring it that way himself in the light of what lay between him and Tuebelo. It even began to seem now, from where Caltraine stood, as though Alred—not the straw boss— had hooked up this betrayal . . . perhaps for the bounty Flake had hoisted on Tuebelo.

Well, the first round was over but Flake would never leave it there. It might take a while but you could damn well bet that before another sun got up he would have what was left of that posse piling in here.

Caltraine, peering at the carnage around him, knew he'd be a fool to hope to hold them off again. Next time that bunch was going to look where they were shooting. Luck was a fickle goddess at best and he had already used up more than his share.

Choking down his nausea, he scrabbled around until he found another rifle, scowled again at the nearest body and forced himself to go through its pockets on a hunt for shells which he did not find. His stomach wouldn't stand for poking round on another. He stripped this one of shell belt and holster and went up the passage, hoping for a horse but not really counting on it.

After rounding the second bend in this labyrinth he began scuffing around for the pitch knots they'd abandoned. He located one but it felt too used up to be any good to him. He struck a match and found the other. In its wavering light he pressed on as fast as leaden legs would take him.

Pretty soon Flake would have that posse on his heels. The man was too impatient to be put off for long with Wolftrap's water all that stood between himself and dreams he evidently cherished. Any man who'd kill a woman and coolly hang it on a friend was damned well capable of just about anything.

Of course all he had was the girl's word for it and she was pretty cool herself when you took a good hard look at her.

It was one of those things you weren't too apt to notice with her right there in front of you. Woolling this around he recalled her spoken readiness to part with half Joe's spread as bait calculated to clinch getting the rest of it. And that business of making out to be tied up and, when that hadn't worked, barreling past on that horse to give him the chance that had put down Alred. Determined, mule stubborn, and reckless to boot.

The sooner he got clear of her and out of this whole feuding end of the cactus the better, Caltraine told himself. With half the tin in the Territory after him, no one but a half-assed fool would let himself get harnessed to slugging it out with the kind of John Law who aimed to look like a cattle king.

With the back door closed he'd have to get out the front, and this was the goal he anchored his mind to. If he got out of this cavern it would be his first intention.

But Terry wasn't that easy to put out of mind. She'd

never stand aside to let him ride out of here. Not if she could help it.

Caltraine paused for a moment to throw a stare across his shoulder, mouth squeezing tight when he caught the sound of horse hooves. He couldn't gauge in a place so mixed up with echoes how much of a lead he might have on those yahoos, but however far back, they were too close for comfort.

24

He wondered again what implied promise or supposed relationship had put that cheated look on Ruddabaugh's cheeks when Terry'd passed him over to name Vic Walters ramrod. In the jumble of thoughts churning through his head was a new curiosity about Terry's mother and a wonder at what old Ambruster was doing about his stage duties if he was down on his back while the girl was away.

None of these things appeared to have much bearing on immediate problems but a man couldn't shut off his mind like a faucet; the deeper one got into this sorry business the bigger the girl's share appeared to be getting. Wherever he turned her hand was before him.

And she was ahead of him now—which could damn well account for the absence of Alred's horse and rifle. Maybe Alred, too, if she had found some way to fit him into her need. Perhaps the fellow had only been pretending to be killed but Caltraine, considering, refused to believe this. He had seen the bullets strike.

The sounds of pursuit hadn't got any nearer but they hadn't quit, either. He could still hear them back there picking their way through the dark on tired horses. They weren't likely to quit with Ben Flake behind them but maybe he could stretch out his lead a few rope lengths.

With this thought in mind he set up his torch in a crack between rocks. He'd been aware of its hazard ever since he had lit it, but knew without it he would have to trust memory not to get himself lost. He could only count on the posse's wanting to comb the surroundings with considerable care before letting Flake push them into its light.

He must be halfway through this labyrinth now. If he could keep out of sight for a little while longer there was at least a slim chance he'd be out of this bind. There would still be Tuebelo, the kid and Bedderman, but he could worry about getting around them when and if they turned up. He didn't think the girl could get back with them before he got out of here.

He quickened his pace, stumbling along with one hand to the wall. If he was able to get out he could stay with the creek till it reached the basin, screened by the growth along both banks. He kept peering ahead for some break in this blackness, some evidence he might be nearing the hole he'd come through getting down here.

The incline got steeper. Twice his hand plunged off the wall into space with an abruptness that left him drymouthed and trembling. Each time lighted matchsticks showed him the tracks he must follow.

As he continued to climb a picture of the man he was charged with killing came to turn his lips thinner. The thing had been smoothly engineered to produce the desired result. Caltraine had been dealing. The man had called him a cheat and, with other men reaching, Caltraine had shot out the Rochester lamp. He remembered the table going over as men kicked back their chairs, the smells of oil and burnt cordite, the shouts and wink of muzzle lights as the thunder of guns beat across that black room.

He'd got out through a window, not waiting for anything. He'd kept away from his lodgings till he could learn what the score was, found it spread over the next morning's papers, himself named as killer with ten thousand dollars offered, alive or dead.

There had been no mention at all of the governor but Caltraine knew Broach's hand was behind it. The dead man had been an important rancher but it wasn't his heirs who'd put up that money and you could be mighty sure there wasn't *nobody* going to trace it back to Broach.

Caltraine pushed on doggedly, eyes straining for a break in this coal-pit dark. Once he imagined he heard the distant bawling of cattle and wondered if he was becoming delirious.

He thought: *What am I here for?* but knew too well the answer to that. He was here because he'd been a damned fool.

He never should have let that girl talk him into this. Should have taken Wong's grubstake and cut for the hills. Those faraway ones to the south. From then he might somehow have slipped across the border where Broach couldn't touch him.

Caltraine, who had never yet lied to himself, grimly snorted. The thought was bitter enough to make even fools laugh. Sure, they'd welcome him all right—for as long as he was able to keep paying off.

He would have to find somewhere else to hole up, by himself, for he could trust no one else. But first he had to get out of here. Abruptly, he heard that cow sound again, the lowing of restless disgruntled cattle, too plain this time for further doubt. Ten stumbling steps later he saw a blue grayness in the darkness ahead.

His mind was too fuzzy, too cluttered with confusion, to

draw any sense from the presence of cattle till he hit the last climb which went up that steep pitch to a hole filled with moonshine. It was the smell of them maybe, perhaps the push of night air, which suddenly froze him into his tracks as comprehension began to unfold.

As piece by piece locked snug into place he saw Tuebelo's strategy plain as the black strokes put on a tally sheet. It was Tuebelo himself who had arranged for Alred to tip off the sheriff.

Deliberately Tuebelo had sent Alred to Flake to show the man how to get into his hideout, glom onto that water and, presumably, lay by the heels not only Tuebelo himself but all the lesser fry with him.

Wolftrap. By God, this place had been rightly named!

Likely Tuebelo, too, had tipped off Flake to Joe Ambruster's intention to visit town that night, thus permitting the sheriff to set up the deal which had left big Tuebelo with the outfit's brass collar.

Then the girl had shoved into it, briefly threatening all the man's calculations. Till he'd hit on this scheme. With the minor refinements already in motion it would take care of everything—Caltraine, too, if he didn't get himself out of here!

With toes dug in, he went scrabbling crablike up the long ramp of talus that led into this maze of subterranean corridors he'd tackled hours ago with such a fine lease on hope.

He caught a grip on the wall, shaky, gasping in the sweat of his exertions, staring into the silvered splendor of the night outside, engrossed in the spectacle spread before him. The cows were there right enough, flanked by the dark shapes of silhouetted riders.

Four, he counted. Two of them off yonder squeezing the herd in his direction, the other pair back there pushing up stragglers. One of those four had to be Terry Ambruster —which meant Tuebelo had even pulled off whoever had been staked out to watch the front door.

You didn't need any crystal ball to see this whole sequence must have been planned before Alred had gone to make his cute squeal to the sheriff. There hadn't been enough time to round up a herd and have it bunched out there, pointing straight at the target, since Caltraine had slapped the girl's horse on the rump.

This whole thing had been hatched behind that black stare of Tuebelo's to rid the world of the man who had made him an outlaw, to get Flake no matter who was killed doing it. He meant to run that whole herd hellbent down this ramp!

25

Caltraine, thinking of Ben Flake, shivered. But the man had only his own mad greed to thank for the destruction about to be let loose. No one had appointed Caltraine his keeper. Yet the thought of such carnage as Tuebelo intended was not to be stomached if a man could circumvent it.

Those possemen with Flake were more dupes than henchmen and, though Caltraine had dropped a couple when his life was the price of Christian squeamishness, he could not in good conscience abet an avalanche of cattle or stand idly by while Tuebelo vengefully loosed a stampede.

Still undiscovered, he crouched with his scruples in the mouth of the cavern opening, trying to think of some way to avert this slaughter. Sometimes running cattle could be turned by a matchflame but he strongly doubted it would be enough in the face of Tuebelo's aggravation.

The man was back there in the drag with the girl popping a rope's end to close up the stragglers. Any wink of light coming out of this tunnel was more like to draw fire than block his intention.

The sounds of pursuit had grown louder back in the depths of the labyrinth behind him. It was when Caltraine remembered the pitch knots piled at the bottom of this ramp and, with no time to lose, whirled about to spring toward them and lost his footing.

Thrown off balance, he went down heavily, wrenching his side, rolling over and over like a torn-loose tumbleweed, unable to stop till he struck flat against the bend of the wall below the ramp.

It was the nearing sounds of Flake's posse that roused him.

Struggling painfully up, he felt around in the murk trying to locate the knots till finally, in desperation, he struck a match and saw them. He'd kept hold of the rifle but his pistol was gone, lost out of the holster. Someone shouted behind him and, snuffing the match, he whirled aside as a gun went off, the slug ricocheting with an angry whine through a racket of shouts breaking out from above.

Through the arguing mumble of voices behind him, Ruddabaugh's shout and a yip-yip-yipping came down from above through a flutter of tarps and the popping of pistols. A tremor ran through the rock underneath him and with no time left he caught up an armful of knots from the floor and plunged toward the ramp.

The accelerated rumble of those churning hooves beat against his ears like a pound of surf with the frightening knowledge he had lost his chance, that the cattle would be on him before he was halfway up. Nor could he hope to outrun them. He was caught in this mole's maze like Flake's posse behind him.

Wind ran heavily out of him. His chest pushed against the bind of damp cloth as he reached for new breath, the outraged inner self of him galvanized to quivering fury by the prospect of leaving his bones in this catacomb. The clamorous dark was no insurance against the sea of horns sweeping toward him and he was suddenly cold despite the sweat on the hand grimly locked to his rifle.

How many loads did it still hold unfired?

Not enough, he knew. He flung himself through the treacherous black toward the shelving wall at the chamber's far end, hanging onto the knots and the rifle as he went scrabbling up the rough scrape of moist stone.

He was stopped at ten feet by the immovable arc of downsloping roof, the whole wedged-in length of him quivering and shaking as he put fire to the pitch knots and dropped them, watching one after the other lift its flickering light to illuminate the thundering avalanche now being funneled through that hole in the cliff.

In the deafening din the sweaty, fear-crazed herd came jostling, wave on wave, down that breakneck ramp. He was triggering the rifle long after its action had cooled to futile clicks, but the barricade of grotesque piled-up shapes—though they snuffed half his torches—shunted the herd on by, sending it raucously off into the black labyrinth of passages below.

Though it seemed an eternity, how long he clung to the face of that wall with those steers thundering past he had no way of gauging; he must have passed out before they were gone. When at last he grew conscious of being still among the quick it took more effort than a man would suppose to unlock his grip from the cracks and convolutions of that ungiving rock.

It was as if every muscle had rooted itself there and his joints felt like they had been in plaster casts. He couldn't think which was the most unnerving: the thunder of those stampeded cattle or the tomblike hush that surrounded him now. Except for the occasional far-off bawling of some lost steer the cavern was still as the dawn of time.

He found it grisly work maneuvering himself across that dead meat and was glad to put the nauseous smells of the place behind. There was no use looking back there for survivors. Trapped by the dark in that crazyquilt of corridors it was highly unlikely anyone had escaped. Whatever strength he had left, he had better conserve for what was waiting outside.

He had used his last match to light the pitch knots that were now unfindable blobs of cooling ashes. He had a belt half filled with cartridges for the six-shooter he no longer had, an empty rifle these wouldn't fit, and a rekindling spark of dogged tenacity whose only goal was to get himself out of here and lost from all knowledge of everyone encountered.

He had no idea how this could be managed. Plans were fruitless till he knew what he was up against.

Near the top of the ramp he threw away the rifle, afterward wondering what the hell he had been thinking of. Shrugging finally, he hauled himself on toward the black rimmed patch of stars ahead, knowing that if Tuebelo was out there waiting, an out-of-fodder Winchester was the last thing a man ought to have in his hands.

Not that empty hands would curb that bird!

If Tuebelo was waiting it would be to polish off survivors.

In the fading moonlight, so far as he could see, the range loomed empty. Though he combed the dark spots time and again before moving out of the cavern's protection, his eyes found nothing untoward or alarming. The whole push had cleared out. There was nothing to hear but the chirping of crickets.

If Tuebelo felt that sure of himself it seemed pretty unlikely he'd have posted a guard on the rimrocks south of the shack. If a man could get past the house unnoticed he stood a pretty fair chance of getting clear of this place.

It was worth a try, anyhow.

Though he ached in every joint and sinew and ought by rights to be totally exhausted, he was surprised to find a new spring in his step. The cold night air was clearing his head and, with hope creeping back, he set off toward the springs, knowing gray dawn to be just around the corner. Already the stars were not near as bright as they had been.

It was an eerie feel to be abroad in this stillness, thinking of men who'd never know this cold again. He found it hard to believe Ben Flake was dead, though he knew the man had to be, caught in the rush of the stampeding herd.

He approached the springs with all the stealth he could manage, but need not have bothered. Nobody was there. It was light enough now to see the going-away tracks of the outfit's four horses overlaying the churned ground pocked by driven cattle.

He struck out along the creek, presently moving into it, glad to be covered by the growth along its banks; and got to wondering about the girl. Was she Tuebelo's prisoner or staying with him by choice?

She had switched sides so often, the only thing a man could really believe was that she'd do whatever at the moment seemed most likely to further her chances of emerging mistress of Wolftrap.

As he drew nearer to their headquarters he grew increasingly cautious. One thing bothered him particularly. Near the buildings, if he remembered right, this creek was in plain view from the rimrocks. It wasn't likely Tuebelo would have seen any need to have a man up there now that Ben Flake was out of the running.

Thing that stuck out was that it wasn't so much the front door they'd be watching as routes one might take across this basin to get there. Though Caltraine put his mind to it, he did not latch onto any kind of helpful notion. If Tuebelo had someone up on the clifftop, there just wasn't any way to get through that slot without being spotted.

26

The wet glimmer of sunlight off the water swirled and
sparkled like a hatful of jewels, but did little to soften
Caltraine's brooding look.

Not for a moment was he about to believe Tuebelo was
fool enough to let anyone clear out. They all knew too
much now to be trusted—and that went for the girl as
much as Bedderman or Ruddabaugh. And he certainly
wasn't going to hug or kiss Vic Walters, whom he probably
imagined had been trampled into doll rags.

Trying to fit himself into Tuebelo's boots made it reasonably clear the man would not let any of them out of his
sight. In which case, like enough, the whole push would be
up in those rimrocks. The man would not risk making any
move at all until convinced the stampede had got the job
done.

Lowering his butt onto a rock sticking out of the stream,
to catch what rest he could while still hidden, Caltraine
found his thoughts once more begin to put up pictures of

the girl. What kind was she, and why was this spread so desperately important?

Weighing all he had seen, reviewing her actions, he came up with the feeling that she had a bone-deep drive and need for the solidness and permanence which to her represented security.

She'd got it into her head this place should be hers and no expedient would be left untried which held any promise of getting it for her.

Though skeptical about her willingness to share it, he surmised she would if she couldn't do better. He continued to sit there sizing her up while the sun moved higher across a white sky toward a rack of clouds darkly looming behind those slate colored Mexican mountains.

He'd be a fool to go farther with that sun blazing down. Be smarter to give Tuebelo time to get careless. Right now he was probably up in those rocks with a glass focused into these hills hunting movement. Caltraine figured those low hanging clouds meant a chance of rain and he'd better wait for it. He remained on the rock, soaking up sun, watching swirls of light skittering across the moving surface of the water.

Sharp twinges in his side—the kind a man will get sometimes from too much running—caused him presently to take a look at his wound, but there was no blood showing. He reckoned it was the hunger gnawing at his gut, that the lethargy he felt was the result of over-exertion. At least the giddiness was gone; that was something to be thankful for.

He didn't know or wouldn't admit why he found it imperative to go out the way he'd come into this place. He didn't owe the girl a thing, but the grind of his thoughts kept turning her up.

Maybe at last he was getting some sense. People learned from experience, if not by example. She could probably turn mean if it happened to suit her, for despite her kittenish prettiness she would do whatever she figured she had to, and to this extent would have to be considered in whatever course he finally hit on. Hardly a woman you would care to have to trust.

Staring into the water as he turned these things over, he must have looked for ten minutes at the pebbles beneath it before something about them caught at his attention. Even then the significance of that dull sheen eluded him. It wasn't till he thrust down an arm and fetched up a handful that a building excitement began to pump through him. Even then he was loath to trust the evidence of his eyes until he'd rubbed a couple of them hard across the rock's rough side.

Gold, by God! Two of these nuggets were big almost as walnuts!

So that's what was back of all the hurrah about this basin.

Small wonder Ben Flake had been allergic to prospectors! If Wong, the Pine Knob storekeeper, had got wind of this—*and he might very well have*— it explained his alacrity in grubstaking a man he must have guessed was on the run.

Caltraine dropped the nuggets back into the water.

He sat on through another long interval until hoof sound pulled him out of his absorption.

The sun had gone behind a scud of lowering clouds and across the dun grayness beyond the fringing willows he saw the shapes of four riders moving deeper into the limestone hills. He saw the hatless girl and, beyond her, Tuebelo's big shoulders and craggy profile, with Ruddabaugh and Bedderman behind them.

They were going to be passing less than forty yards away.

Caltraine knew the risk of moving but was plainly astride the horns of a dilemma. Unarmed as he was, if they swung over here and discovered him, he'd be shot on the spot. He would not be left loose, you could damn sure bet on that!

Joint by joint, Caltraine came off the rock, lowering himself into the thrust of water behind it, submerging until only his head showed.

It was soon enough evident they were drawing nearer.

"Kid—" Tuebelo growled just when Caltraine thought they were about to ride past, "get over and cut for sign along that creek. If anyone got clear we don't want 'em gettin' by us."

With the clump of Ruddabaugh's mount seeming almost on top of him, Caltraine was seized with an impulse to jump the man and was still gripped by it when, filling his lungs with a last gulp of air, he dropped below the surface.

When he couldn't stay under even another split second he put up his head to see Ruddabaugh pushing back through the willows. "Nothin' there," he heard Ruddabaugh call.

It was hard, when he pushed himself up to stand there emptyhanded, to watch those ponies ridden off out of sight. But he'd had no real chance of getting one of them.

Nor was it comfortably easy to put that girl out of mind.

She had looked to be with them of her own volition— and maybe she was, but it hadn't been her that was giving the orders. And Tuebelo, already charged with the death of one woman, wouldn't hang any higher if he got rid of two.

27

Caltraine understood what gold could do. It could twist people's minds into condoning almost anything and very likely was the key to contradictions in Terry's character. He couldn't doubt it was the basis of her obsession with Wolftrap.

It gave a greater credence to Flake's machinations and pretty certainly was the answer to the pushy dominance of Tuebelo, and the steps he had taken to insure he stayed topside in this deal. Gold could buy him a place in this country, which was still sufficiently lawless for wealth to hoist an umbrella of virtue. It could laugh off charges leveled at him by a crooked sheriff no longer around.

Caltraine had a clear track now through that slot. And the means. There'd be horses penned at Wolftrap headquarters and no one to stop him making use of a couple. There would also be grub—perhaps even a firearm. So what was he waiting for? It was still a long walk and he had better get at it before Tuebelo and company put in another appearance.

The girl, after all, was not his concern. There had never been any relationship between them; she was not his responsibility. She'd come into this deal with both eyes open and her part in that set-to with Hobey Alred revealed a considerable ability to look out for herself. He'd piled up enough grief in her behalf. It was time to dig for the tules if he didn't want his scalp hung up in Broach's office!

The shank of the afternoon was not far off when, rimming out of the arroyo, he got his first close stare at Wolftrap headquarters. There was no sign of movement. The place looked as deserted as he had every right to imagine it was. But, still with mixed feelings about Terry Ambruster, he took the time to look it over pretty thoroughly before tiredly limping toward a pen which held three nickering horses.

One of them had lines that suggested speed and bottom, the other two were average, but after what he'd been through he was not at all inclined to quarrel with their appearance. He stepped across to the barn and fetched back a bucket of oats after peering to make sure there was water in the tank.

Then he headed for the house with a feed sack he'd picked up to look for a gun and see what supplies were available. Midway across the yard he looked over his shoulder one final time but saw nothing he hadn't seen the last time he'd turned. Tuebelo, he guessed, would be hunting that money belt he thought was around the middle of a dead Vic Walters.

This picture triggered another thought. When Tuebelo didn't find it, wouldn't the man's suspicions swing against the girl?

Uncomfortably Caltraine backed away from visions conjured by so sharpened an insight. With mounting irritation, he tramped on toward the house.

Rounding its corner to come at the door he suddenly

stopped short, arrested by the sight of a horse primly tied to a bush just beyond the shut door.

First off it came over him one of that bunch had slipped back here for something, but this wouldn't wash—he'd never seen the horse before.

A lot of wild thoughts splintered through his head as he stood there cocked on the balls of both feet. With hand clenched futilely against empty hip, his hardening stare whipped across saddle leather without seeing a thing he might use for a weapon.

The fact that this rig held no boot for a rifle was no guarantee the bloke wasn't holding one. If Caltraine tried to run he could be shot from a window.

"All right," he growled with all the authority he could give it, "you coming out friendly or do I go in there after you?"

For a long dragged-out moment there was no sound at all. Then the door latch was lifted, the door slowly opened and the Pine Knob merchant, Mr. Wong, stepped reluctantly into the overcast light.

A look of astonishment abruptly lengthened the storekeeper's face. Something moved through those almond shaped eyes like doubt; then, with his whole stance relaxing, he stepped nearer to catch up Caltraine's hand and pump it.

"Mr. Walters!" he cried, standing back to peer again. "Is this *really* you?"

"Sometimes I'm bound to wonder," Caltraine muttered. "What are you doing out here?"

"Old Ambruster's dead."

For a couple of moments, Caltraine gawked stupidly.

"I thought Miss Ambruster ought to know about this," Wong said nervously.

Caltraine, looking at him, nodded. Though it did seem a little fortuitous that out of sheer neighborly interest a man with his own established business to keep an eye on would come such a piece to so bullet prone a community as Wolftrap.

"How'd it happen? Someone stick a gun in his ribs?"

"Nothing like that. Doc seemed to think it was something he'd eaten. Like it didn't agree with him."

Caltraine said, eyes dark with new thinking, "Didn't you tell me the girl had been taking care of him?"

"He was not a well man . . . been up and down all summer. Something to do with his heart, I believe." Glance drifting across Caltraine's empty holster he said with less than total persuasion, "He'd been up and around . . . he was down at the store for some ammunition—"

"When was that?"

"Just before she left to come out here."

"How'd you know she'd be coming out here?"

"Where else would she go?"

They looked at each other through a moment of silence. "How did you know she had gone?" Caltraine asked.

"It was Wednesday night that Ambruster came in. Always on Thursday . . . Are you trying to tell me she isn't here?"

"She's here," Caltraine said. "What did Ambruster want with those cartridges?"

Wong stared blankly, not saying anything.

"Did he seem in good spirits? His usual self?"

"More quiet, I thought."

"Like there was something on his mind?"

"There may have been."

"Did he know about his son being killed?"

Wong, silent a while, said thoughtfully, "I don't believe Miss Terry would have told him . . . not before she left anyway."

"Did you know her mother?"

Wong shook his head.

"Ever hear where she came from?"

"I believe Mr. Ambruster made her acquaintance in the Kentucky Bar. I've heard she used to sing there."

"You don't think he bought those cartridges with some crazy idea of avenging his son?"

"It hadn't occurred to me."

"He could have heard about Joe from somebody else."

The storekeeper shrugged. "Ambruster wasn't killed by a bullet."

"The news about Joe wouldn't help a bad heart." Caltraine pulled up his head. "How did you know the girl wasn't home?"

"On Thursdays she always came in for groceries. When she did not turn up either Thursday or Friday—"

"You remembered Ambruster's quietness and those bullets he bought."

"Yes," Wong nodded. "I wondered if he'd got out of a sick bed to buy them. I went up to the station. The girl wasn't there. The old man was dead. After the doc had gone off with the body—"

"Shh!" Caltraine flung up his hand.

Through a tightening moment they listened to horse sound.

Caltraine whirled to the window over the sink, all his thoughts spinning down a long darkening spiral. The girl and three others were fanning into the yard, Tuebelo out front with the grin of a cat below those cold eyes.

28

Tuebelo's look raked the yard one last time, slewed round to touch the girl; then, his voice came hard at the house. "All right, Walters—we know you're there."

Caltraine realized too late his own tracks had found him for them.

Clenched fists revealed the frustration rocking through him. If he hadn't fooled around here gabbing— He was stuck in this bind, caught flat-footed without even a pistol and not the ghost of a chance of reaching those penned horses.

He looked desperately at frightened Wong but found no bulge of a hidden gun. One slim hope filtered through his churning thoughts. The door of this shack faced away from the yard and outside the door, concealed from Tuebelo, Wong's mount was tied.

He called through the window. "What do you want?"

Sitting his horse in bullypuss triumph the straw boss grinned.

"Just get shucked of those guns and come out with your paws up."

"What would I want to do that for?"

"Come on—come on," Tuebelo growled, impatient. "You put up a fight you won't *never* get outa there. By God, this time we've got you dead to rights!" he rasped, chuckling.

The fact was self-evident.

Even if he got a leg over that horse he hadn't one chance in twenty of clearing this yard before one of those shooters loosed a slug with his name on it.

Caltraine licked at cracked lips. You couldn't make much of a fight against three jaspers with guns. The thing he was trying to decide was if he stepped out would that be the end of him? Was he going to walk slapdab into a slug? Outside were men wholly capable of trying that—young Ruddabaugh, for instance.

But Ruddabaugh wasn't calling this tune. And if Tuebelo was after the gold in that creek it didn't look like he'd try anything quite so crude. He didn't have to. An "accident" could take care of Walters. The man could arrange to get him thrown off a horse. Or have someone drop a rock on him.

What it all came down to, though, was that Caltraine didn't have any choice. "All right," he called out, turning, brushed past Wong and stepped through the door.

He strode round the corner without so much as even glancing at Wong's horse, knowing if he did he might have second thoughts. He stopped perhaps forty feet from the house, the others coming up to him, the girl peering hard, darkly expressionless, Tuebelo still with that grin on his mouth.

"Well, well," he said with derisive satisfaction. "A Prescott killer with ten thousand on his pelt don't look no different than any other slob, once you've drawed his stinger and got his hands above his ears. You can put 'em down now, Caltraine.''

So they knew who he was, and had probably known for some while.

Caltraine, with cold prickles running up and down his spine, gingerly lowered his arms, seeing behind an impassive face the blood money lust twisting Ruddabaugh's features as the kid slid down across the leathers of his saddle. Behind him Bedderman sat with white fists tightly wrapped about the horn.

Tuebelo, dismounting, never taking his eyes off Caltraine for an instant, came up and put a hand out. "Thought maybe you'd like to have this for a souvenir."

On the callused palm of that spread-open fist gleamed a crumpled bit of metal that once had been a star. Poking it into Caltraine's shirt pocket, the straw boss said: "I'll take that belt now, killer."

Caltraine stood cold as a lump while Tuebelo, reaching inside his shirt, yanked open the buckle and stepped back with the belt. Then Tuebelo rasped, "I could eat a damn buzzard—wings, beak an' all! Get in there, girl, an' scrounge up somethin'."

She looked from one to the other, before reluctantly climbing from the saddle. Caltraine could almost taste the fear that had hold of her. This was rampant enough even for a brute like Tuebelo to notice. With his stare cutting round, the man laughed. "He'll be all right. Get on with it, woman!" Then to Bedderman, he commanded, "You go on in there with her. Make sure she behaves."

The flustered Bedderman almost fell off his horse in anxiety to prove his heart was in the right place. Ruddabaugh showed a flash of rabbity teeth and got himself braced to go after Caltraine again, but Tuebelo packed it up before the young fool got his mouth halfway open.

He brought a hand down decisively. "Never mind that! I'll do any windmilling Wolftrap stands in need of."

Whatever notions Caltraine had half formed on the unsuspected presence of the storekeeper in that cabin went gurgling down the drain when Bedderman was sent hotfooting after Terry. He had nothing left now to count on but his fingers.

Tuebelo, eyeing him, expansively chuckled. "Going to be some changes made in this country. Be a lot of arched backs before this gets done with and mister, you're just what the old doc ordered. Somethin' to work their mad off at." He threw back his head with a belly-shaking guffaw.

When no one else laughed he said like they were stupid: "Christ!" and spat, settling his scornful look on the kid. "Turn out these nags and put them saddles on some fresh ones, and catch up one for loverboy here too." He jerked his thumb in Caltraine's direction. "Well, what you waitin' on? Heard me, didn't you?"

He stood hard eyed till Ruddabaugh, scowling, grabbed up their mounts' reins and wheeled off toward the pens. "And don't take all night, either," he called after him.

Good nature restored, he rubbed a mocking stare again over Caltraine. "Hell, it's simple as slobbers. Here we've found in our midst a real killer, son of a bitch that's diddled the governor, varmint with ten thousand tacked to his scalp—skunk who'll try anythin' to get out from under.

"Now you take Ben Flake. He wasn't what a man could rightly call popular but he was all the law we got in this country. Pine Knob ain't much, neither—kinda down at the heels, but they got their pride and they're strong for their own." A grin spread his lips. "You begin to get the drift?"

When Caltraine refused to unbutton his lip Tuebelo asked, "How you think they're going to feel when I show up with *you* and they find out their sheriff took a posse out here—on a tip from a man you killed—to pick you up while we were busy with roundup, and before they could get out of that passage you wiped out the whole push with a stampede of cattle?''

Caltraine, braced for trouble, had been holding his breath. Confronted with a strange horse bush-tied by the door of a shack supposedly empty even Bedderman, you'd think, would have got off a shout or made some sort of commotion.

The continued eerie quiet from behind those walls had been working on his nerves like a blacksmith's rasp; but now—with the gist of Tuebelo's cunning beginning to filter through—Caltraine stood frozen, his thinking processes paralyzed by those grinning words.

Tuebelo, moving the wad on his jaws, said, "What kinda odds you give yourself now, killer?"

29

A few large drops fell out of the leaden sky over their heads but neither man lifted his stare off the other. Though Caltraine had never lived easy, he looked about as near this time to the end of his string as a feller could get and still be aware of it.

Tuebelo and the dark worn butt of that gun on his thigh were just enough out of reach that any lunge leveled at him was foredoomed to failure.

The straw boss chuckled. "Man kind of looked for bigger things from you."

"You'd like an excuse to bust a leg for me, wouldn't you?" Caltraine scrubbed at the itch of sweat-dampened whiskers. "How you figure to keep me from talking when you hand me over to that lynch mob in town?"

Tuebelo hauled a fold of paper from his vest, shook it open to disclose a sketched-in face below black type that cried: *$10,000 REWARD.* "Talk all you want," he invited affably.

It didn't look a heap like Caltraine's own conception of himself, but no one was likely to quarrel with that after Tuebelo's version of the facts was fed to them.

The man said smugly, "Who you reckon is going to believe you?"

No one, probably. Caltraine could see that. And the reward was just as good dead as alive.

The reward was, sure, but his value to Tuebelo as distraction and scapegoat would lose most of its merit if he had to be fetched into Pine Knob dead.

This was something to work with but you didn't have to be dead to be secured from escape. The straw boss had only to shoot a leg out from under him.

What the hell was going on in that cabin? he wondered.

Ruddabaugh came up with the fresh mounts he'd been sent for. "Smells good," he said, lifting his nose toward the shack. He dropped his reins on the ground and considered Caltraine, scowling. "If we're goin' to pull out why be bothered with him—he'll pack just as good dead."

"You're too young to understand the fine points of Tuebelo's strategy," Caltraine said. He grinned at the kid the way you'd look at a moron, then said to Tuebelo: "They might see things some different if they got wind of that gold."

It was a calculated risk which he knew might well push Tuebelo into shooting him out of hand. But he had to do something. With the kid continuing to back Tuebelo's play there was no chance at all of Caltraine getting clear. He had to drive some kind of wedge between them and reckoned he had done it when he saw the shocked flare that widened Tuebelo's look.

The whole length of the man rocked back on his bootheels but this was lost on Ruddabaugh, who was staring openmouthed at Caltraine. "*Gold!*" he cried. "What the hell you talkin' about?"

The kid started toward him. Tuebelo's words slammed into him harshly. "Stand back, you fool! Can't you see what he's up to?"

Ruddabaugh stopped in confusion but the whirl of his thoughts began to heat with greed and his eyes, now openly suspicious, riveted on Tuebelo's face.

"Tell me," he said through unmoving lips.

"He's trying to turn you against me—" the straw boss began, but the kid's fist dropped around his gun butt.

"Never mind that. Let's hear about this gold."

Sweat rolled down Tuebelo's cheeks. "For Chrissake!" he growled. "It's just something he's made up—"

"Maybe I made these up, too," Caltraine drawled, and held out a palm on which two nuggets dully gleamed.

The kid was still staring at them when Tuebelo shot him.

Whirled half around, Ruddabaugh, face contorted, tried desperately to bring up his gun. On buckling knees, he got off one load that flung up dust from the ground in front of him. Fire leaped again from Tuebelo's middle and, as the kid jerked and toppled, the sweep of his pistol sent the nuggets flying out of Caltraine's hand.

Jumping back as the girl and Bedderman came running round the cabin's corner, Tuebelo rasped above the snout of his weapon: "Get back in that shack—you, too, mister! And if you open that trap again," he snarled at Caltraine, "I'll break both your arms an' work you over for good measure!"

30

Man, believing what he wants to believe, finds it hard in the bind to recognize himself as the victim of hallucinations, and this is doubly true where the cherished illusion—however remotely—appears to have held out the promise of salvation.

There was no horse tied to the bush by the door and no trace of Wong as Caltraine, holding his still numb wrist, followed Terry and Bedderman inside. Tuebelo, tramping in their wake, kicked the door shut. Shoving Caltraine savagely into the wall, he grabbed the gun from Gurd's holster with a livid fury that left each of them rooted in their own fears.

"Now get this straight," he snarled with the words scarcely louder than their heartbeats. "There ain't going to be but one boss to this deal. Like that goddamn Ruddabaugh, you've all had your notions, but unless you're craving a dose of his medicine you'll jump when I say jump! *Is that understood?*"

Each of them probably had private reservations but nobody was doing any sounding off about it.

"There ain't nobody slick enough to cross me up an' hope to get away with it!" His black stare passed from face to face. "Now get that grub on the table," he told Terry and, yanking open the door, still holding Bedderman's six-shooter, he went outside.

The overcast sky in this windless light had an olive tinge. Caltraine, grimacing, thought of the tracks Wong's horse must have left. His scowl touched the girl. Terry, face unreadable, began dishing up.

Considering Tuebelo's reaction to those nuggets, Caltraine was persuaded to reassess some of his thinking. Way it looked now Terry'd no idea there was gold on this spread; her consuming interest must have sprung full-blown from a woman's natural need of security, sharpened perhaps by the life she had known as an unwanted child. As ward of her stepfather—himself without prospects—she had had to make her own way in a man's alien world.

Crossing behind her, Caltraine moved to the sink to have a look through the window, drawn by the clatter of metal on stone. Both the straw boss's hands, when he came into view quartering toward the face-down lump of the kid, were empty.

The girl, peering round Caltraine's shoulder, remarked, "Looks like we're all in the same leaky boat. You got any ideas?"

Caltraine shrugged. "Not really. Last time a country got yellow like this we had one hell of a blow, if you'll pardon my English."

For a girl, he thought meanly, there was always marriage. . . . But who could she meet in an out of the way place like Pine Knob? And if she didn't think first of herself, who else would?

Tuebelo now was bending over the kid. A whistling wind

picked up dust from the horse pens and fanned it, skirling, across the yard. Tuebelo's unfastened vest, turned hair side out, was blown over his left shoulder and his hat went kiting as he rose out of his crouch with Ruddabaugh's shooter, dumping its shells, to send it skittering into a growth of brush beyond the barn.

The room was filled with the sound of her murmur. "You see what I mean? He doesn't overlook *anything.*" She grabbed Caltraine's arm, shaking it angrily. "You haven't been hearing a thing I've said!"

"Where's Wong?" he asked harshly, jerking free of her.

"I've sent him to Pine Knob for help—"

"After what happened to Flake and that posse you expect to get any help from there?"

Rain, coming suddenly down in sheets, drummed against the tin roof. He saw Tuebelo, hatless, running for the house and caught the blurred tag-end of some blacker darkness dropping behind the gray metal rim of the farthest pen's horse tank.

Before he found words the drenched bulk of Tuebelo lunged to a stop in the open door, hanging there like the shape of disaster with his slate colored eyes taking everything in.

"Where's that goddamn Bedderman?"

The startled girl wheeled to look, but as Caltraine had just now discovered, the timid crewman—taking advantage of their preoccupation—had slipped out and decamped.

"He can't have got far—" Terry nervously began, but the black look striking from Tuebelo's face brought her hand against her mouth, the words dying behind it.

"If this is some of your doin', you been wastin' your time," Tuebelo snarled. He came, dripping water, pulling a chair to the table. "Soon's we've ate we're gettin' the hell out of here."

Filling his plate with the lion's share, he sat down to the business of putting it away. Caltraine sat down across from him and Terry came over with the pot to fill his cup.

Looking up out of the sides of his eyes, Tuebelo suddenly erupted from the chair, getting out of the way the split fraction of a second before the scalding contents of that upended pot could accomplish the girl's intention. Face twisting with rage, his left fist lashed out in a backhanded blow that flung her reeling against the sink.

Caltraine heaved the table hard into him, diving across its inch-thick top to take the man off his feet in a floor shaking fall. But Tuebelo, a veteran at this kind of fighting, crashed his head into Caltraine's face, the shock of this impact roaring all through him.

Before he could catch up the slack in his grip, Tuebelo had both thick arms wrapped around him. Caltraine, unable to break this hold, desperately rolled across the floor, but the clamp of those arms inexorably tightened. No spine could long withstand such pressure. Caltraine brought a knee up into Tuebelo's crotch, heard the breath burst from him in an agonized shout. The arms fell away and Caltraine clawed to his feet.

Hard breathing, he watched while Tuebelo, gasping, got his own legs under him. Thus far Tuebelo, confident in his advantage of at least forty pounds, had made no move to get at his gun. But it was only a question of time, Caltraine thought, and lunging suddenly forward he struck him hard on the cheek. With eyes unfocused, Tuebelo whipped up his arms to cover himself. Caltraine knocked them down.

Step by step he beat the man back. Tuebelo stumbled, then got himself braced and, lowering his head, bored in, half bent over. He grabbed Caltraine at the chest, hauled him off his feet and slammed him furiously against the wall. Caltraine half fell, still fighting for air.

Groggy with punishment, he saw the dense shape of the man closing in, and struck blindly. The blow rolled off Tuebelo's shoulder and his hands lifted Caltraine again, flinging him murderously into the stove.

Caltraine yelled as the searing bit of hot metal tore through him. Then he shoved himself off in a reflex of agony and his buckling legs dropped him, twisting, on the floor. Instinct made him try to bring up his knees as Tuebelo's panting shadow loomed over him. A cold wind fanned across the room, damp with rain. Suddenly the girl's frightened shout rang through Caltraine's groggy mind.

He tried to push himself up, finding no sense at all in her panicked cry of *Ben Flake!* Thinking she must have gone off her rocker, Caltraine was astounded that it *was* Ben Flake crouched in the doorway. And looking very much alive, thin lips stretched in that saturnine leer as he savored—across the gleaming line of a leveled rifle—their ludicrous expressions.

Tuebelo stood fast, both big fists empty, frozen off balance in his look of malevolence like some atavistic relic from the dawn of time.

Whatever dark plans ran through Flake's head, his trust in that rifle was a fatal mistake. Caltraine, cocked and gathered on the balls of his feet, flung himself doorward as the galvanized straw boss, faced with the ruin of all he had schemed for, exploded into action.

Two shots rang out, monstrously banging off the shack's wooden walls. Flake rocked back, all his joints loosening as Caltraine wrenched the heavy Winchester from his grasp.

Tuebelo's gun barked again and a white shocking impact slammed Caltraine headfirst against the doorframe. Shoving himself off, he staggered round through the racket of that flame-sheathed pistol and squeezed the rifle's trigger.

The last thing he saw as the fog closed about him was the disbelieving stare of Tuebelo's eyes.

The next thing he recognized, from flat on his back in a lumpy bunk, was the girl's concerned face. Made him wonder for a moment what it might be like waking up every morning with the same one beside you.

He looked up at her, aghast, cold sweat breaking through the pores of his skin. He thought he must be a heap worse off than he'd imagined to let a fool notion like that latch onto him.

He tried to get up but her hands wouldn't let him. She bent nearer. "Take it easy," she said.

She didn't have to worry about the man he'd made look foolish. "I've got to be riding!"

"How far do you reckon to get with that hole in you?"

"That ain't the point. You don't understand. When that bunch comes from town I've got to be out of here—"

"You mean on account of that card party killing Broach used for an excuse to hang ten thousand round your neck?"

He looked at her, shocked. "You figuring to turn me in for the money?"

"It's you who doesn't understand, I'm afraid. They're not looking for you any more." She pushed the hair off her cheek. "The killer confessed."

He found this hard to take in. "*When?*" That single word was harsh with suspicion.

She said, smiling slightly, "I believe it was about a week ago."

Caltraine scowled and reckoned he had cause to be pretty riled. "Then you knew when you hired me . . .?"

"Of course. Wong recognized you. He'd just come back from Prescott. When Flake's outfit cut Joe down in the street he said I was going to have trouble with Tuebelo. He suggested I grab you and—"

"Is that why he gave me that grubstake?"

"That's right," she nodded. "I agreed to pay him back when I came into Wolftrap."

"I sure been played for a ninny!" Caltraine said bitterly. "What's happened to my belt and that stake I had in it?"

"I've got that, too."

When he growled, half suspecting, "What do you mean by that 'too'?" she said, openly laughing, "I've got *you*, haven't I?"

Caltraine, tiredly sighing, smiled and closed his eyes.

*   *   *   *   *

Nelson Nye was born in Chicago, Illinois. He was educated in schools in Ohio and Massachusetts and attended the Cincinnati Art Academy. His early journalism experience was writing publicity releases and book reviews for the *Cincinnati Times-Star* and the *Buffalo Evening News*. In 1935 he began working as a ranch hand in Texas and California and became an expert on breeding quarter horses on his own ranch outside Tucson, Arizona. Much of this love for horses can be found in exceptional novels such as *Wild Horse Shorty* and *Blood of Kings*. He published his first Western short story in *Thrilling Western* and his first Western novel in 1936. He continued from then on to write prolifically, both under his own name and the bylines Drake C. Denver and Clem Colt. During the Second World War, he served with the U.S. Army Field Artillery. In 1949–1952 he worked as horse editor for *Texas Livestock Journal*. He was one of the founding members of the Western Writers of America in 1953 and served twice as its president. His first Golden Spur Award from the Western Writers of America came to him for best Western reviewer and critic in 1954. In 1958–1962 he was frontier fiction reviewer for the *New York Times Book Review*. His second Golden Spur came for his novel *Long Run*. His virtues as an author of Western fiction include a tremendous sense of authenticity, an ability to keep the pace of a story from ever lagging, and a fecund inventiveness for plot twists and situations. Some of his finest novels have had off-trail protagonists such as *The Barber of Tubac*, and both *Not Grass Alone* and *Strawberry Roan* are notable for their outstanding female characters. His books have sold over 50,000,000 copies worldwide and have been translated into the principal European languages. The *Los Angeles Times* once praised him for his "marvelous lingo, salty humor, and real characters." Above all, a Nye Western possesses a vital energy that is both propulsive and persuasive.